About the author

Eoin Colfer is the author of the best-selling Artemis Fowl series and the critically acclaimed WARP series, as well as many other titles, from picture books to novels for adults. In 2014, he was named Ireland's laureate for children's literature. He lives in Ireland with his wife and two sons.

To learn more about Eoin Colfer, visit his website at

WWW.EOINCOLFER.COM

#MarvelYA #IronMan #TheGauntlet

MARVEL

IRON MAN

THE GAUNTLET

Other Books by Eoin Colfer

AIRMAN

HALF MOON INVESTIGATIONS

THE SUPERNATURALIST

THE WISH LIST

ARTEMIS FOWL

ARTEMIS FOWL AND THE ARCTIC INCIDENT

ARTEMIS FOWL AND THE ETERNITY CODE

ARTEMIS FOWL AND THE OPAL DECEPTION

ARTEMIS FOWL AND THE LOST COLONY

ARTEMIS FOWL AND THE TIME PARADOX

ARTEMIS FOWL AND THE ATLANTIS COMPLEX

ARTEMIS FOWL AND THE LAST GUARDIAN

ARTEMIS FOWL: THE GRAPHIC NOVEL

ARTEMIS FOWL AND THE ARCTIC INCIDENT: THE GRAPHIC NOVEL

WARP: THE RELUCTANT ASSASSIN

WARP: THE HANGMAN'S REVOLUTION

WARP: THE FOREVER MAN

MARVEL

IRON MAN

THE GAUNTLET

EOIN COLFER

EGMONT

EGMONT
We bring stories to life

This edition first published in Great Britain in 2016 by Egmont UK Limited,
The Yellow Building, 1 Nicholas Road, London, W11 4AN
First printed in the United States of America in 2016 by Marvel Press,
an imprint of Disney Book Group
This book is set in Perpetua. Designed by Tyler Nevins.

ISBN 978 1 4052 8541 4
66752/1
Printed in the UK

For Seán, as promised

A modern-day warrior mean, mean stride,
Today's Tom Sawyer mean, mean pride.
– **Rush**

THE BIG IDEA

Los Angeles, the 1980s – which were not as bad as people think

Tony Stark paced the lacquered wooden floor outside his father's office, chewing one stick of gum after another. For three hours he'd had to hang around waiting for a meeting with his own dad.

It was ridiculous.

Forcing your only son to wait on a sunny day was, the teenage Tony felt sure, against some universal good-parenting guidelines. Especially since Tony was about to change the face of Stark Industries forever. All his life Howard Stark had griped that nobody ever brought him the *big idea* and he had to think of everything himself. Now Tony had that big idea in his backpack, and dear old dad was making him wait while he had lunch with the baby-faced governor of Arkansas.

Howard Stark's secretary, Annabel, sat behind her glossy wooden desk without offering so much as a word of sympathy, or even a glass of water. In fact, the only thing she sent Tony's way was a disapproving glare so heated that Tony felt it was interfering with his elaborate hairstyle.

'Come on, Annabel,' he said. 'Ease up on the daggers. You're melting my head.'

Annabel did not ease up. If anything, her glare grew more intense, and she added a curled lip to the expression.

Tony felt he should challenge this blatant antagonism. 'Is this about Cissy? Is that what this is about?'

Annabel snapped a pencil between her clenched fists. 'My daughter's name is Cecilia, not Cissy.'

'Hey, she told me Cissy, and I was not about to argue with such a pretty girl. She told me Cissy, so I went with Cissy.'

Annabel jumped on that. 'You went with her, all right – down to the beach in the middle of the night.'

'It was nine thirty,' said Tony. 'I wanted to show Cis– *Cecilia* the dolphin that swims into the cove. That was it. Nothing happened. The dolphin didn't even show up.'

'Maybe nothing happened,' conceded Annabel, 'but you have a reputation, Tony. Every mom in Malibu has your name on her watch list.'

'Come on,' objected Tony. 'I'm fourteen. Harmless.'

Annabel actually snorted, which was new for the

normally demure secretary. 'Harmless? Boys like you are never harmless. You are the opposite of harmless.'

'That would be harm*ful*,' said Tony, who had never learned the talent of keeping his mouth shut, even while chewing gum.

'That's right,' said Annabel. 'And maybe you haven't done any harm yet. But you will.'

Tony was a little stunned.

He had been in this outer office maybe a thousand times, and all Annabel had ever said to him was 'Good morning, Master Stark,' or 'I'll tell your father you're here, Master Stark.'

Now it was all laser eyes and insults. Could it be that Annabel had a point? Could it be that he, Tony Stark, boy genius and all-around charmer, was actually harmful in some way?

Every mom in Malibu had his name on a list?

They would soon cross his name off that list if they knew what was in his backpack.

'Cecilia is a great gal,' he said, giving some of his all-around charm a try. 'I would never harm her.'

Annabel straightened some papers on her desk that already looked pretty straight. 'First,' she said, 'don't call my daughter a *gal*. This is twentieth-century California, not the Wild West. Second, maybe you won't harm her, but you probably won't call her, either. That's how cruel boys like you operate, isn't it, Master Tony?'

Tony squinted suspiciously. When Annabel called him

Master Tony, it did not sound like she meant *Master Tony*. It sounded like she meant exactly the same thing that his mom meant when she called him Anthony, which was pretty much the same as his father meant when he called him anything – as though every variation of his name was an accusation of something.

Tony!

Anthony!

Master Stark!

All disapproving.

Tony could hear his father's voice now.

'Tony! Get your head out of the clouds.'

Actually, he *could* hear his father's voice as Howard Stark, back from his three-hour lunch, steamrolled through reception, the customary thunderhead scowl pasted on his face.

'Tony, let's go. This better be good, because I don't have all day.'

Tony hitched his backpack a little higher.

'It's good, Dad. Real good,' said Tony, thinking, *He's gonna make me partner when he sees this*.

'It better be,' said Howard Stark, pushing through the double doors into his office. 'Annabel, hold my calls,' he said over his shoulder, then added, 'for three minutes. Shouldn't take more than that.'

Tony swallowed. It would take him two minutes to get the device set up. That left one minute for the pitch.

He squared his shoulders.

One minute is all you need, boy genius, he thought, and he followed his father into the office, or, as the employees of Stark Industries referred to it in whispers, the Lion's Den.

Howard Stark was not a fan of Californian architecture. Floor-to-ceiling windows were not his thing. In his opinion, more looking out meant less looking in, which for years Tony had thought was stating the obvious, until he realized that by 'looking in' his father meant *thinking* or *inventing*.

Having said that, his dad was doing his share of *looking out* right now, staring at Tony as though he were an alien who had just come through a wormhole.

'What the hell is that?' he said eventually, pointing in the vague direction of his son's head.

'That's my head, Dad,' said Tony. 'And this Q&A is not coming out of my three minutes.'

'Not your head, Tony. The thing *on* your head. Are you wearing a wig?'

'A wig?' said Tony, injured. 'Come on, Dad. A little gel, maybe, but not a wig. This is the latest style. There's an English band called Duran Duran; maybe you've heard of them?'

'No, I have not,' said Howard Stark, settling into his leather office chair. 'Modern music is just old music dumbed down for a dumb generation – though that governor guy blows a pretty mean saxophone, they tell me. He'll be president one day, mark my words.'

When other people said 'mark my words,' it was a kind of vague prediction not to be taken seriously. When Howard Stark said it, it meant he planned to use his fortune and influence to make whatever event he had marked happen, and you could bet your last dime on its coming true.

Mr Arkansas doesn't know what's about to hit him, thought Tony.

Howard was not finished with his hairdo lecture. 'I bet that style you've got going there takes, what, an hour to get right? That's an hour of gaping at yourself in the mirror. Looking *out*, Tony. Looking out, when you could be looking *in*.'

'I *have* been looking in,' said Tony hurriedly, eager to stop this style lecture in its tracks before his three minutes were up. 'And I've come up with something.'

Howard crossed his arms and grunted softly. The message was clear: *I'll believe that when I see it.*

Yeah, well, you're about to see it, old man, thought Tony. *Prepare to experience the awe.*

And while he shrugged off his bag, he also thought that as soon as he was partner he'd be able to say that kind of stuff out loud.

Tony laid the bag on his father's desk, then unzipped the main compartment. He reached inside gently, as if to cradle a newborn kitten, but what his hands came out with was a small flying machine with a bulbous nose and two sets of low-slung wings with inset rotors.

'I know what you're thinking,' he said. 'A model aeroplane. Big deal, right? But this is so much more than a model.'

Tony was prepared for his father to be unimpressed. What he was not prepared for at this point was for his father *not* to be unimpressed. Or rather: impressed.

'Wait a minute,' said Howard Stark, literally jumping from his chair. 'Wait just one minute, young man.'

Howard Stark hurried around the desk and grabbed the plane right out of Tony's hands.

'This is …' he said, turning the craft over in his hands. 'I don't believe this. Have you been in my files? The battery, the cameras …'

Tony pulled the miniature plane from his father's grasp. 'No, I haven't been in your files. This is all me, Dad. One hundred percent Tony. I call it the *Tanngrisnir*, which was the goat that pulled Thor's chariot. Not that I believe in any of that stuff, but I needed a name, and I know you like the Greek classics.'

'Norse,' corrected Howard absently. 'Thor is a Norse god, but never mind that now. How did you put this together?'

For a second Tony's usual stream of patter dried up, because it seemed as though the moment he'd dreamed about for so many years (i.e. impressing Pop) had finally showed up, and now that it was there, he didn't want to blow it.

Three minutes, he told himself. *Get cracking.*

'I combined all the traditional sensors for weight efficiency. Magnetometers, gyros and accelerometers, in one little box.'

'I see,' said Howard, taking the *Tanngrisnir* gently from his son. 'You did all this at home?'

'Yes, in my room.' This was not as tough a task as it sounded, because Tony Stark's room had more tech in it than most universities. 'The brain is a tiny embedded computer, which I control with this.' Tony pulled a grey box from his pocket. 'This is a prototype of something called a Game Boy. It's not really your thing, Dad.'

Howard surprised him. 'Nintendo's revolutionary gaming device. That's not even coming out for a couple of years. How did you get hold of it?'

'I have my sources, Dad,' said Tony mysteriously. 'I modified the program, boosted the output and – here's the clever part – linked it to a communications satellite so I can fly the TOT – Tony's *Tanngrisnir*, that is – halfway around the world on one battery charge. And what the TOT sees, I see on this dinky little screen. What do you think?'

Howard Stark's features aligned themselves into an expression Tony had never seen before.

Was it?

Could it be?

Admiration.

Maybe there would even be a hug? The first one since he'd turned ten.

'I am impressed, Tony,' said Howard finally. 'You've saved me eighteen months on our drone programme with this combination sensor alone. All this time we were working in parallel, and I never knew. That is inefficient resource management. I need to pay closer attention to your work.'

Being labelled a *resource* to be *managed* was not exactly the warm embrace Tony was hoping for, but it was infinitely preferable to being ignored completely.

Howard Stark tugged his glasses from his breast pocket and studied the cargo bay. 'Just one question for you.'

'Sure, Dad, fire away.'

'That's kind of the problem. I don't see a mount for the missile ... Or is the TOT itself the missile?'

Tony frowned. 'Missile? Dad, there's no missile. The *Tanngrisnir* is a delivery system for medical aid. With the TOT I can drop malaria vaccines into a war zone with no loss of life. I can flit over minefields with a microcargo of penicillin or blood plasma. With a thousand TOTs I can avert a famine from my bedroom.'

Tony activated the Game Boy and flew his creation right out of Howard's hands.

'Look how maneuverable it is. That's because I used rotors and wings. The TOT can do anything, Dad. This is our chance to move away from weaponry. This is Stark Industries' chance to do something good.'

Howard's face hardened, and Tony knew he'd blown it.

'*Something good?* Something good, you say? So keeping this country safe isn't a good thing?'

'No, Dad, that's not what I meant.'

'Because the only reason you can sit in your bedroom single-handedly averting famine is because I keep your bedroom, and this entire country, safe.'

The hoped-for hug seemed very far away now. 'I know that, Dad. I know you do.'

'And still, knowing that, you waltz in here and casually suggest that it's time for Stark Industries to do something *good*.'

Tony felt his heart sink. He had been so close to breaking through his father's barriers. But with a few badly chosen words, he had raised those barriers to an all-time high.

'Dad, listen ...'

But Dad was not in the mood for listening. He was in the mood for delivering another lecture.

'Tony, what you fail to understand is that ...'

We are at war, thought Tony, his heart sinking even further.

'... we are at war,' said Howard Stark, right on cue. 'And just because you can't see the enemy does not mean that they are not out there.'

And I just bet me and my hippy friends are blind to the dangers.

Howard Stark was on autopilot now. 'Of course, you and your hippy friends have no idea what's really going on.'

Tony attempted an intervention. 'Dad, no one even says the word *hippy* anymore.'

Howard steamrolled over him. 'No, no. You'd much prefer to fritter away the freedom that I provide by finding ways to undermine me. Coming in here with this gadget to save Stark Industries.'

Tony brought the TOT in for a landing on his father's desk. 'Forget it, Dad. It's just a toy. It doesn't matter.'

Surprisingly, something Tony said seemed to penetrate. '*A toy?* Just a toy . . .' Howard held out his palm.

'Spit,' he ordered.

Maybe this is code for something, thought Tony.

'Spit,' said Howard again. 'The gum. Now.'

What could Tony do but obey? He spit the gum onto his father's palm.

'A toy, you say,' muttered Howard, his hands busy with the TOT. 'Let's see what our enemies can do with a toy.'

'Dad, I get it, okay? There's no need to freak out.'

Howard laughed. '*Freak out*, Tony? Nobody says that anymore.' He rummaged in his desk and found what he was looking for, then stuck it to the bottom of the TOT with the blob of chewing gum.

'Now, let's see, let's see,' said Howard, almost feverish in the throes of his demonstration. 'What have we got? What do we have?' Tony's father went over to his small bulletproof window, opened it and gazed into the parking lot. 'Yes, there it is. My DeLorean. I love that monstrosity, Tony, love it. But let's send it back to the future, shall we? Why not?'

And he tossed the TOT outside. A year's work, right out the window.

'Dad!' shouted Tony, rushing to look. But his father held him back.

'You better get flying, Son. Tick-tock.'

Tony whipped up the Game Boy and managed to take control of the TOT an instant before it crashed into the parking lot's asphalt. Even from a dozen floors up they could hear the craft's motors whine in protest at the rough handling.

'Well done,' said Howard, and some part of Tony appreciated the rare compliment even in a moment already jam-packed with emotions. 'Nicely handled under pressure. And there will be a lot of pressure when you're averting famine and so forth. But not crashing is the least of your worries. The *mission* is your priority, and in this case your mission is my DeLorean. Everyone in that car has been affected by a fatal virus, and your little plane is carrying the antidote. But this is a time-sensitive mission, Tony. You need to land the TOT on my DeLorean's roof in thirty seconds, or everyone in that car is dead.'

Tony wasn't sure what was actually going on. Was this a real test, or just a lesson? Either way, he was not going to fall at the first hurdle. Or second hurdle, if you counted the expert and cool way he'd regained control of the plummeting TOT.

Land on the DeLorean, he thought. *No problem, Pop.*

Tony knew exactly where the DeLorean DMC-12, with its distinctive gull-wing doors, was parked: in the executive section of the lot, far away from the riff-raff's cars. He quickly nudged the TOT in that direction, pulled up the nose twenty degrees to give the camera a better view, and made a looping approach from twenty feet off the asphalt.

'Better not scratch the car, Son,' said Howard in his ear. 'That's my favourite vehicle.'

Which was saying something. Howard Stark had something of an obsession with cars, but John DeLorean was the only automotive engineer he was on record as admiring. And if Howard Stark admired a person, then that person was doing something very right.

So what was all that talk about sending it back to the future? And what did Dad stick to my TOT? The weight feels a little different.

It was another test, he decided.

Pops is piling on the pressure by throwing off the TOT's balance.

Good luck with that.

Tony had been practising for weeks with the Game Boy in preparation for exactly such a baptism of fire, and he felt pretty darn confident in his piloting skills.

I could land this baby on a playing card, he thought. *Setting her down on a luxury sports car will be zero problemo.*

Tony had enough smarts not to smirk. If there was anything his father hated more than his son's hairstyle, it was his irrepressible cockiness.

I will smirk later, Tony decided. *And* maybe *punch the air. I might even call Cissy.*

But later for celebrating. Now for landing.

The DeLorean grew large on the screen, and Tony glanced quickly at the sensor readouts to make sure the TOT was not going to be buffeted by wind, but conditions were perfect. Even the sun was playing along by staying offscreen.

Ten feet, thought Tony, holding the craft steady. *Five.*

A crazy thought flashed across his mind, something crazy thoughts often did.

I should do a barrel roll.

But good sense prevailed, and he opted instead to expertly execute a gentle vertical touchdown. A textbook landing, no cockiness whatsoever on display.

Or at least a gentle vertical touchdown was what he'd *intended* to expertly execute, but an instant before the aluminium landing skids could seesaw onto the DeLorean's hood, Howard Stark closed his hand over those of his only son.

'Dad, don't!' objected Tony, attempting to pull away, but the strong fingers held him fast.

'Watch and see,' said Howard Stark.

Tony could do nothing but obey, and he watched as the TOT's pointed nose dipped sharply, scraping a long groove in the DeLorean's paint.

'You're doing this, not me!'

'Don't worry,' said Howard Stark. 'It's just a toy, remember?'

Tony wriggled his fingers out from under his father's, abandoning his grip on the Game Boy. He ran to the window just in time to see his precious TOT nose-dive into the windshield of his father's even more precious DeLorean.

He winced but was not overly concerned. After all, from that distance, how much damage could a featherlight craft do? Even one with chewing gum stuck to its cargo doors.

As it turned out, the answer was quite a lot.

Like most explosions, it was over before the brain got a chance to process what had happened. But when Tony replayed the incident in his mind, slowing it down to view it frame by frame, he remembered an ultrawhite flash followed by a roiling ball of flame about the size of a cantaloupe from which the DeLorean's windshield seemed to recoil like a membrane before shattering into countless pieces (technically not countless, if you're being picky) and then the entire hood crumpled as though stepped on by an invisible iron boot.

At the time, all Tony could think was: *I hate cantaloupes.*

He would continue to hate them for the rest of his life and never consciously realize why.

Then the sound wave hit the building, followed by

heat and the cacophony of concentric circles of car alarms.

In the grand scheme of explosions, this one was nothing special or major. Certainly not special enough for Howard Stark to be called on to explain personally. Big enough to send a security guard down if a police car showed up, perhaps, but there would never be so much as a noise pollution fine as a result of Howard's demonstration.

Whatever that demonstration was supposed to prove, thought Tony. *Aside from the fact that my dad loses it on occasion.*

Which was a surprise to absolutely no one in the compound.

Tony was surprised to feel a hand on his shoulder.

'Do you see, Tony? Do you?'

Tony did not see, and he was not about to irritate his dad with wild guesses.

'I don't see, Dad. I don't. You melted my flying machine and your favourite car.'

'Correct,' said Howard. 'Because a picture paints a thousand words, and a picture of an explosion paints a million more.'

'I still don't get it. The TOT was an instrument of peace.'

'Exactly,' said his father. He turned Tony away from the window, stooping to look him in the eyes. 'It took you a year to build that drone, and it took me ten seconds to weaponize it with some gum and a mini-grenade, because you told me all I needed to know. Don't give away your secrets, Tony – not to anybody – or they will inevitably turn them against you, as I did.'

Tony wondered later why his father kept mini-grenades in his drawer and whether that was even legal.

'Why would you want to do that?'

'Because that's what we do. We men. We make weapons. Everything we build is on its way to becoming a weapon, and only a fool or a child does not see that. If we put your mercy plane into the hands of our enemies, they will fly it back to us bearing a payload. Do you understand?'

Tony did, but he didn't like it and said so.

'You don't have to like it,' said his father. 'You just have to remember what you've seen here and accept it as the way of this world. There are no toys in this world, just unevolved weapons. The weapon will always be our greatest achievement.'

Tony glanced once more through the window at the narrow plume of blue-black smoke rising from the DeLorean's engine block.

'I will never forget what you showed me here today, Dad,' said Tony, and he meant it. Maybe his dad's methods were a little out there, but he sure could get his point across.

'Good boy, Tony,' said Howard Stark, handing his son the Game Boy. 'Someday you'll take over this company, and it will be up to you to keep this country safe. You won't be able to do that with toys. Got it? Promise me now that you will continue my work when the time comes.'

Tony gazed down at the game device in his hand and knew instinctively that a defence contractor somewhere was already adapting the technology. Probably Stark Industries.

'I promise, Dad,' he said. 'No toys, just weapons.'

And if he had to pick a moment when his childhood ended, that would have been it. Followed closely by the moment two weeks later when both his parents were killed in a car accident on the Pacific Coast Highway.

Tony Stark never looked at toys the same way after that. For years he wouldn't play with any at all. And when he did eventually begin to play again, he studied his old building sets and physics kits with hardened eyes. Tony Stark worked on his toys until they were of an altogether more dangerous kind than the ones of his youth.

His new toys were armoured and explosive and they could fly. In fact, they weren't toys anymore; they were weapons.

2

PROTOTONY

Twenty feet above the Irish Sea, present day

Tony Stark dreamed he was flying. But it wasn't just any flight of fantasy. It was a very special flight over the Hawaiian volcanic peaks with a very special, very beautiful woman: Anna Wei. Lithe, strong and brilliant, she was the only other scientist he had ever considered his equal, and one of just a handful of people Tony had ever loved. And like all the other people Tony had loved, Anna had died before her time. After the police found and identified her body, they ruled it a suicide. As much as Tony had not wanted to buy that, he'd had no choice. His heart had hardened a little more that day, and he'd resolved never to love again.

So Tony Stark dreamed he was flying, and the fact that he dreamed he was flying while he was actually flying added an extra dimension of reality. The previous Iron Man operating system had once put forward the hypothesis that one more layer of dreaming could prove inescapable. In other words, if Tony dreamed that he was dreaming he was flying while he was actually flying, then he might never wake up. At which point Tony had decided that the OS needed a reboot and maybe a virus check.

Tony's current onboard AI was his girl Friday, who was a little more free-spirited and knew better jokes and even occasionally laughed at Tony's.

Friday woke him with a gentle vibration that massaged his spine, which she detected from his bio readings was about to spasm after many long hours of flying across the United States and the Atlantic Ocean.

Stark opened his eyes and yawned and, feeling his chin nestle into the helmet's jaw strap, remembered he was in the suit.

'Morning, Friday.'

Friday winked into existence in the form of a holographic red-haired young woman, who was crystal clear even in full daylight thanks to the Stark multinode projectors. Right now she was confined to the helmet display, and Stark knew that if he focused on her for too long, he would throw up in the helmet. But even out of the corner of his eye, he noticed something.

'You've changed your hair?'

Friday shook out the long red tresses that had been shorter the day before.

'That's right. This is more me.'

Friday had changed a lot of features lately. The whole Irish thing, for example. Friday had been programmed Californian but had turned Celtic in the past few weeks. Also, Friday's virtual bone structure had changed so her face had more character. Tony was intrigued to see what the AI would do next. He had built Friday, but she was intelligent and could choose to appear as she pleased.

'Where in the world are we?' he asked the artificial intelligence.

'Twenty minutes out, boss. Heading north northeast one mile off the Irish coastline.'

'How are the systems looking?'

'All the readings are in the green, appropriately enough, considering where we are,' said Friday. 'And top of the morning to you.'

'Top of the morning?' said Tony. 'Friday, I never took you for a stereotype. What's next? A pint of Guinness and some Riverdancing?'

'Just trying to get into the swing of things, boss,' said Friday. 'Ireland, I have decided, is my spiritual home. And I don't think *Riverdancing* is an actual verb.'

'Increase lumbar vibration to four,' said Tony. 'And throw in a stretch, why don'tcha. I know I look as cool as all hell, but these transatlantic jaunts take it out of a fella.'

Friday took hold of Tony's spine and pulled till it

creaked. 'Maybe if you took any notice of international law and didn't do so many uncleared flights, Tony, your back would be in better shape.'

Stark ignored this. 'Don't we have a first-class Iron Man suit? Didn't I build something with a minibar?'

Friday laughed. 'We have recycled water and caffeine patches, boss. I'm afraid that's it.'

Tony grimaced. 'Recycled water. I know where that water came from and it's putting me off, to be honest. And getting back to the transatlantic flights, there are a lot of big weapons in the hands of bad people, and someone's got to clean it up, right? If S.H.I.E.L.D. won't sanction my missions, then I gotta strap on the stealth suit and do it myself.'

Tony thought back to a recent meeting with S.H.I.E.L.D. during which Nick Fury had made it abundantly clear that he was not about to rubber-stamp Tony's covert missions.

'You must be out of your playboy mind if you think I'm going to ask the president to green-light your Boy Scout trips,' the S.H.I.E.L.D. leader had yelled in his office at S.H.I.E.L.D. HQ. 'You think you're God, Stark? You think you can make up for fifty years of Stark Industries' manufacturing weapons by deciding who gets to have tech now? That ain't how the universe works, Tony. You should know that. You're a genius, right? You've told me so enough times.'

And Tony had said, 'Yes, Dad.' Which had been more

than embarrassing; it had been mortifying.

'Did you just call me *Dad*?' Fury had asked, wickedly delighted. 'Let me get the S.H.I.E.L.D. psychiatrist in here. I think you might be suffering from some kind of genius-level PTSD.'

'I was being sarcastic, Fury,' Tony had said, trying to cover for the slip. 'As in, you are not my dad. And you are not the boss of me.'

'You're wrong there,' retorted Fury, pounding his desk – which was, Tony thought, a little grandstand-y. 'I *am* the boss of you. And if you get yourself in hot water during one of your escapades, don't expect S.H.I.E.L.D. to send in the cavalry, because I ordered you not to go in the first place.'

Tony Stark left Fury's office realizing that not only was there no backup forthcoming, but he would have to be a lot sneakier in the future when he was taking down arms dealers, because Nick Fury would be waiting for him to slip up.

Luckily, thought Tony as he flew above the choppy surface of the Irish Sea, *one of the facets of my genius is definitely sneakiness.*

'Friday,' he said, 'how's my yacht doing?'

Friday brought up the yacht's locator and hummed as she checked it – an endearing tic she had developed herself.

'The *Tanngrisnir* is at anchor one mile outside the mouth of picturesque Dún Laoghaire Harbour, as programmed,' replied the suit's AI.

'Done Leery,' said Tony, sounding it out. 'The Irish sure know how to spell things. You can never have too many silent letters, right?'

'Watch it,' said Friday. 'Those are the physical manifestations of my people you're talking about. Any more insults and I might send you for a swim.'

'Any pings on the boat?'

'Two S.H.I.E.L.D. sats and three helicopter fly-bys from news networks. Judging from the chatter, all seem satisfied that Tony Stark is getting a little R&R with Shoshona Biederbeck, the world's newest pop superstar.'

'Why wouldn't they be satisfied? It's a totally believable story: Tony Stark with a beautiful woman.'

Friday made an unconvinced kind of sound, a little like a single note from a clarinet.

'What's that supposed to signify, Friday?' Tony asked. 'Are we doing noises now?'

'I am an intelligence, boss. You do want honest opinions, don't you?'

'I do. But I prefer actual words – you know, verbs and nouns and so forth – over beeps and honks. What are you, Artoo-Detoo?'

'Well, if you must know, Shoshona seems a little young. Twenty-five at most?'

Tony laughed. 'Are you jealous of a robot, Friday?'

'No. Jealousy is certainly outside my program parameters. I am concerned with the sustainability of your cover story.'

'First, I think you've been outside your program parameters for weeks now and second, I worked a long time to make the "beautiful young woman" cover realistic. Any other worries while we're on the subject?'

Friday made another clarinet sound, which turned the helmet display pink for a second.

'Mood lighting,' said Tony, delighted. 'Maybe we should play some disco music. Come on, Friday. Out with it.'

'Well …'

'Well? Well? What is happening to you, Friday? Are your language patches disintegrating?'

'It's just that I know how touchy you are.'

'Tell me. That's an order.'

'Very well, boss, but you pushed me into it, so don't get mad.' Friday took an audible deep breath, which she accomplished by flushing the suit's vents, a little humanizing trick she'd come up with herself. 'It's the Prototony.'

'What's wrong with the Prototony?' asked Stark. 'That thing is a marvel of modern engineering – and pretty darn good-looking, too.'

'I'm not disputing the engineering of the Prototony, boss.'

'So, what is it? You have a problem with his appearance?'

Another honk, followed by, 'Well …'

'Well what?' asked Stark. 'Come on, Friday, you're

killing me.'

'Well, he's a little buff.'

'Sure, he's buff. I'm buff. And he's supposed to be me. S.H.I.E.L.D. and the tabloids spy on the Prototony, which leaves me free to do my little side missions. Never be where you're supposed to be, remember?'

Friday persisted. 'If he's supposed to be you, then maybe he shouldn't be so muscular. I mean, you're in good shape, boss, don't get me wrong, but your shape is documented. And the Prototony's shape is a little more *developed* than yours.'

'I'm not exactly the Hulk, is what you're saying.'

'I knew you'd be angry.'

'I'm not angry. A little peeved, maybe.'

Friday tittered. '*Peeved?* According to my records, you are the first person to use the word *peeved* outside of a romance novel in fifteen years. There should be a prize.'

'So the Prototony is too buff?' said Tony, unwilling to leave the subject. 'Or maybe I'm too puny.'

'I'm sorry I mentioned it,' said Friday. 'My observation is based purely on your muscle mass and BMI, and it wasn't meant as a criticism.'

Tony was silent for a long moment, then said, 'We have EMS on this rig, don't we?'

'Yes, boss,' replied Friday. 'The defib can be used for electromuscular stimulation.'

'Then give me fifteen minutes on abs. I wanna look good for the satellites.'

The electromuscular stimulation had barely finished its work chiseling Tony Stark's torso when Friday sealed the vents and took the suit subaqua so they could approach the *Tanngrisnir* from below. After all, it might seem a little curious if Iron Man touched down on the yacht while Tony Stark was visible on deck. It was a safe bet that Nick Fury would be yelling through the sat phone within seconds of seeing that video. So Tony had fitted out the *Tanngrisnir* with underwater doors and an airlock that could accommodate a billionaire philanthropist genius in a metal suit of armour without raising so much as a ripple, physical or electronic, on the surface.

Tony dodged fish for a while until Friday retook control half a mile out and guided the Iron Man suit into the welcoming claws of the *Tanngrisnir*'s support rig. It cradled Tony like a newborn babe while he was winched gently into the yacht's loading bay.

'Okey-dokey,' said Friday. 'The lotion is in the basket.'

The suit peeled back almost fluidly, panel by micro-panel, until Tony Stark stood exposed in his black unitard.

'Okey-dokey?' he said. 'I don't remember slang being part of your programming.'

'I am an AI, boss,' said Friday. 'Therefore, I learn. What did you think of "The lotion is in the basket"?'

Tony stepped out of the suit entirely. 'I liked it. You took a quote from one of my favourite movies and turned it into a command. Nice. You know something? I really am a genius.'

Friday transformed herself into a glowing life-size hologram in the loading bay.

'And humble, too,' she said.

Tony stretched until his spine cracked. 'No such thing as a humble genius, Friday. All that humility gets you in this world is stepped on.'

'Or happiness and respect.'

This was an unusually philosophical line from the usually bubbly AI.

'I have all the respect I need,' said Tony. 'And I'll be happy when I've taken all the weapons of mass, medium and small destruction out of the hands of people who shouldn't have them.' He rotated his head. 'I am so stiff. People have no idea. They think the Iron Man suit is all saving the world and being cool. And it *is* about those worthy endeavours, but a few hours in that thing is like riding the world's longest roller coaster. I need to loosen up.'

'How about twenty minutes of capoeira before dinner?' asked Friday.

'Perfect,' Stark said with feeling. 'Brazilian martial arts and a steak. Just what I need.'

Friday stepped into the Iron Man suit, closed it up, cued Stark's capoeira playlist through the yacht's sound system, and faced off against Tony.

'Take it easy on me, Friday,' said Tony, limbering up. 'I've had a long flight.'

The Iron Man eye sockets lit up, and Friday's voice

came from the mouth speaker. 'I never take it easy,' she said. 'That's how you made me.'

And for twenty minutes Tony Stark sparred with his own suit in the hidden loading compartment of his multimillion-dollar luxury yacht, which, along with a two-screen cinema and a small nightclub, had enough tech on board to run the Pentagon.

An hour later, Tony watched the Prototony, the android version of himself, fry up a rib-eye in the yacht's galley, which was a galley in name only, as there was nothing galley-like about it. No tight squeezes and cramped cupboards there. The kitchen had three induction rings and two double ovens, of which Tony had only ever used one, to dry out his favourite sneakers after they had fallen overboard.

'You know what?' he said to Friday. 'Maybe the Prototony *is* a little, you know, beefy. It's not attractive, is it? All those muscles.'

'No, boss. Women hate that,' said Friday mischievously from the other side of the table.

'Maybe I'll shave him down a few inches all around when we get back to Malibu. We can say I went on a detox.'

'I will schedule an overhaul,' said Friday. 'Now, if you're going to eat that steak, you'd better get chewing, because we have a party to drop in to.'

At that moment the Prototony turned from the cook-top, frying pan in hand, and said in a fake Texas accent,

'Who's hungry, pardners? If you are, stick out a plate for the best steaks this side of the Rio Grande.'

The real Tony winced. 'Ouch. That accent is terrible. I think old Proto's speech package needs an upgrade.'

Friday disagreed. 'I don't think so, boss. The accent is terrible. But that's how *you* do Texas.'

Tony was surprised. 'Really? Well, if I ever attempt a Texas accent in public, please administer a low-level shock to shut me up before I upset an entire state.'

Friday, being a loyal AI, promised that she would.

The Prototony was not, in fact, a prototype. It was just that the name had stuck from Tony Stark's first attempt to build a replica of himself several versions previously. Other trial names had included the Tonybot, the Replistark and the Toborg, which had been Friday's favourite, as it sounded like an insult somehow. She had even taken to referring to people she didn't like as "total Toborgs". In any event, android Tony swanned around the oceans on board the *Tanngrisnir*, giving the actual Tony a little wiggle room to fly his solo missions to remote and dangerous parts of the world, recovering and retiring stolen weaponry. Much more difficult was creating the virtual pop star Shoshona Biederbeck and making the world believe that she was a real person. Stark had written a program that analyzed the structures and progressions of all the major chart hits of the past half century, and then he'd churned out his own versions of the tunes, which were amalgamations of previous songs – close enough to sound familiar but removed enough to avoid copyright lawsuits. Shoshona's last three videos had exploded all over the Internet, and she had hits like "Bang Boom Pow", "Girls Got the Power", "Oops, What'd I Do?" and the obligatory message track "You Know You're Beautiful, Right?"

The trouble was Shoshona had grown so popular that a music label wanted to meet her, so Tony had to build a convincing Shoshona-bot. It was either that or his songstress would have to go into exile due to the pressures of the biz.

'There is such a thing as being too smart,' Friday often told him. It would have been far less complicated in every way to construct a hologram of a mysterious beauty, but Tony Stark enjoyed playing with the media, so he went the extra mile with Shoshona.

After dinner, Tony retired to his dressing room for a quick cleanup before the evening's party. A local rock band was throwing a launch bash in their city-centre hotel, and Tony had promised to attend in the suit.

Everybody wants the suit, he thought. It was a double-edged sword. Sure, the Iron Man suit was a marvel of technology and a thing of total virtuosity, but sometimes it would be nice to be invited somewhere where the real reason for the invite was not just to get Iron Man to the shindig.

The lead singer, Graywolf, had been a total gent about

it: 'Hey, Tony, brother. Just bring yourself on Friday. No hardware necessary. After all, you have the big gig on Saturday.'

But Tony knew that the guests would be disappointed if he didn't at least do a DJ set in the suit. Throw a little servo into the mix, as it were.

'Are you sure about this party, boss?' Friday had asked him. 'After all, you're speaking at the environmental summit on Saturday in front of some of the world's most influential environmental ministers.'

'That's why I'm going to the party,' Tony had replied. 'I need some fresh happy memories before spending the day with government ministers.'

'I suppose so,' Friday had said. 'Some of those ministers are complete Toborgs.'

But even so, he would not go full tilt on the partying, because the summit was important for the eco-future of the planet, and his keynote speech would ensure that the world's news outlets took notice. Besides, he had quit drinking years before.

So he would strap on the suit for both events.

But not the combat suit. There was zero chance he was bringing that much firepower to any party. And there was less than zero chance that the security details of the various ministers would allow him into a conference wearing the equivalent of a tank on his back. So *that* suit had to stay behind. But not intact. There was no way he was leaving a combat suit on the yacht, even one with the

Tanngrisnir's security system. So he had a couple of jobs to do: (1) disassemble the combat suit and (2) print up a Party Pack.

But before that, it was time to go under the laser.

Tony lay very still on the table.

'Lie very still, boss,' said Friday, operating two robot laser arms bearing down on his face.

'I *am* lying still, Friday. Very still.'

'Stop talking, then.'

'You stop talking to *me*. You know I need the last word.'

'The last word could cost you. These arms are accurate to a dozen or so microns, but if you keep moving ’

'I'm not moving.'

'Stop talking.'

'You stop.'

'I'm powering up now.'

'You don't need to tell me that, I can see the power light. I designed the system.'

'You really need to shut your face, Tony.'

'You really need to stop being rude to your boss.'

'Here we go.'

'Go on, then.'

Two luminous red dots of concentrated heat appeared at the tips of the laser arms.

'Say another word,' said Friday. 'I dare you.'

For once Tony Stark decided to forgo having the last word. He remained perfectly still while Friday shaped his famous goatee, shaving the bristles into straight geometric lines accurate to the nearest ten microns. And if the result was not perfectly symmetrical, it was only because Tony Stark's face was not perfectly symmetrical.

The *Tanngrisnir*'s 3-D printer could print things that made objects printed by other 3-D printers look like they were fashioned by a caveman with a flint axe. Which is a long-winded way of saying that the Stark 3-D Red Special, named for Brian May's famous homemade guitar, was light-years ahead of the competition. Or as Tony himself put it:

What competition?

Which became the most successful marketing slogan in the history of Stark Industries.

There were several things that set the Red Special apart from other printers. For one, it could print from a range of materials, which it could also separate from each other in its recycling smelters. It could print carbon-carbon composites, complex mechanics, liquids, microcircuits, prosthetics, nu-skin bandages, antiaging mud packs and a very tasty pineapple-coconut flavour of Greek yoghurt.

In short, Tony's 3-D printer was every bit the technological marvel that May's guitar had been at the time, and it even sported a similar mahogany trim.

He stood in front of the Red Special now, in the

yacht's lab. The lab was concealed underneath the bottom of a swimming pool that could be raised or lowered depending on whether Tony was working or entertaining. Once upon a time, the z RUN/s ω| needle would have been almost permanently pointed at s ꝏ|. But then Tony spent a little time in an Afghani terrorist camp and his perspective underwent a polar shift. Tony Stark still liked to party, but it was more occasional and often as a cover for some more covert activity.

Tony stood before the Red Special and watched as Friday controlled the winch that lowered the long-range Iron Man suit into the printer's smelter vat.

'Farewell, faithful servant,' he said, always a little maudlin about destroying a creation, even though it was unthinkable to leave a fully operational battle suit lying around on the yacht while he went gallivanting around the mainland. He wouldn't have brought the suit at all had he not needed it for the extended flight. 'It is a far, far greater thing you do now, and yada, yada, yada.'

The suit slid into the large vat, which resembled nothing more than a burger joint's deep fat fryer, and Friday, with her trademark impish humour, had the suit salute on the way down.

Tony laughed and then said, 'I shouldn't be laughing. That suit was a part of me, Friday.'

'Sorry, boss. Don't worry, he'll be up and about again in no time.'

In fact, many of the suit's sections were up again

almost immediately, as the vat's smart gel rejected them and they hung suspended in a servo field in the print matrix. The plates and components were not rejected due to obsolescence or defect but because they could be recycled; it would be an absurd waste of energy to melt down gear and workings just to refabricate identical parts.

While there were many variations on the Iron Man suit, for the past couple of years the basic skeleton had stayed the same. Components such as most of the helmet, many of the superlight nitinol body plates, and the entire spinal section could be reused, along with the propulsion system and jazzy chest light.

After that, things got radically dissimilar, as the Party Pack was a totally different animal than the Battle Suit. Where the Battle Suit had firepower, the Party Pack had bells and whistles. Where the Battle Suit could withstand a sustained barrage from heavy artillery, the Party Pack could withstand a sustained barrage from paparazzi while dazzling the crowd with a laser light show and directional fireworks.

If the Battle Suit could be likened to a pilot's stealth jet fighter, then the Party Pack could be fairly compared to an entertainer's one-man-band equipment, with extra *ta-da!*

There were many advantages to the Party Pack: It was light compared with the Battle Suit. It was decidedly nonlethal, which was a considerable relief to the wearer. It could never hurt anyone, even if it fell into the wrong hands, as the tiny Vibranium battery built into its chest piece had a half-life of only twenty-four hours and the suit was coded to Tony's biorhythms, as were all his suits. It also had air-conditioning and gel packs to cool down Tony's 'poor, traumatized pores' after intense dancing. Friday's words, not his.

'Okay, Big T,' said Friday. 'She's ready to par-tay.'

'That all sounds so wrong in an Irish accent,' said Tony, stepping onto a raised dais at the rear of the lab. 'Never say any of that again. Especially the Big T part.'

He raised his arms and allowed Friday to assemble the suit around him. The entire procedure took almost five minutes, as one of the boots was a little bit off and had to be recast.

'I need to realign the nodes,' said Tony as Friday *manually* shaved the second boot.

'You could print new ones,' said Friday.

'Which would also be off.'

Friday laughed. 'That was a joke, boss.'

'I don't know, Friday,' said Tony. 'I think you're a little giddy. Big T? Jokes? You might need an upgrade yourself.'

'That hurts,' said Friday. 'I'm an AI; we have something approximating feelings. I'm not just some toaster who doesn't take things personally.'

'Yeah,' said Tony. 'Those toasters are heartless beasts.'

'You know what I mean.'

'Yes, I do,' said Tony, flexing his fingers inside the gauntlets, enjoying the power that the tiny servomotors bestowed upon him. 'I wouldn't change a thing about you.'

'Glad to hear it,' said Friday. 'Now, calibration.'

Tony groaned. 'My favourite.'

And for the next ten minutes he performed a number of increasingly complex actions in a set checklist to make certain that the fresh suit was accurately adjusted. To an observer it would seem as though Iron Man was trying to pass a particularly challenging drunk-driving test, which started off with a simple finger on the nose and ended with a triple tuck and roll in midair.

Once that was completed, Tony selected a shortcuts package from the display menu so he could command the suit to perform various manoeuvres by making a simple gesture. His favourite Party Pack shortcut was a double finger click, which would set the suit moonwalking and blast disco classics through the speakers. Always brought the house down, and in a less destructive fashion than Iron Man usually brought houses down.

'Can we please go now?' he asked Friday. 'Those turntables won't turn themselves.'

'That's a roger, Big T,' said Friday. 'We are good to embark on mission DJ.'

'What did I say about Big T?'

'You said to call you Big T at every opportunity?'

Tony smiled. Friday was way more fun than his previous OS had ever been. 'Yeah, that was it. How could I forget?'

Friday opened the internal sea doors. 'All set, boss.

Could I recommend an early night? We have a long day tomorrow. Not that it matters to me; I'm immortal. You, on the other hand, are aging as we speak.'

'Early night it is,' said Tony, ducking into the air lock. 'Three a.m. max. Four at the absolute most.'

'I'll believe it when I see it,' said Friday, opening the external doors and flooding the chamber.

There was no need for a stealth exit, as Iron Man was expected on the mainland, but Tony had long before learned that it paid to be sneaky where the press was concerned. So he peeled away from the yacht underwater and ghosted the surface for a few hundred yards. A quick glance at the heads-up readouts told him that the internal temperature was a comfortable sixty-five degrees Fahrenheit, but darned if the Party Pack didn't always feel a little chilly underwater. He didn't bother mentioning it to Friday, as she would undoubtedly tell him that it was all in his head.

Something else on the heads-up caught his attention: a small screen that was constantly active, cycling through various input sources.

'What was that?'

'What was what?' asked Friday, with exaggerated innocence.

'Come on. You saw it before I did. There was an alert on the weapons scan. Not only that, but we're in the area.'

'It's possible, but we're busy tonight, boss.'

'Cycle it back, Friday. I want to take a look.'

'I don't recommend taking a look.'

'And why's that?'

'Because of your borderline obsessive personality, boss. You can never just *take a look*.'

Tony's voice took on a harder edge. 'Take us to a thousand feet. Put the suit in a holding pattern over the city and give me a look at that report.'

Friday literally could not disobey Tony's angry voice or even waffle a little, as its register was flagged as imperative in her systems. When the audio sensors picked up this tone, the suit went into battle mode – not that battle mode meant a whole lot in the Party Pack, which was armed with fireworks, Mentos and a soda water hose.

Nevertheless, Friday did as ordered and swung the Iron Man rig into a steep ascent, throttling back at one thousand feet. The city of Dublin twinkled below in a hazy network of summer lights, and a gentle wind made the suit's plates hum.

'Show me,' said Tony, still no-nonsense.

Friday enlarged the screen until it filled the entire display. She scrolled back to the clip highlighted by the screening program Tony had devised to sync with most of the earth's sat-cams and search for specific stolen armaments. The clip showed a small island less than eighty miles from their current position.

'Little Saltee,' said Friday. 'Two miles off the south-east coast of Ireland. Uninhabited for the past fifty years.

Used to be a prison island in the Middle Ages. Nothing on it officially except the ruins of an old prison and a bird sanctuary. The island is a nature preserve for over forty types of gull. No humans allowed.'

'No humans allowed officially. What about unofficially?'

'Unofficially I can see a boat docked in the old harbour. There's a camouflage tarp draped over it, but the outline is clearly visible.' Friday zoomed in on the bulky shape in the small harbour and traced a line between several sharp protruding points in the tarpaulin. 'I am fifty percent certain from the profile that the boat is a Stark Poseidon U.S. Special Ops gunboat.'

'Fifty percent?'

'Best I can do.'

'Off the Irish coast? That's a heck of a long way off course. What's she packing?'

'She's rigged for machine guns, mini-guns, grenade launchers and fifty cals. That's a minimum. You could mount whatever you want on those gunwales.'

'Is the source reliable?'

'It's a weather satellite for a French station. I just picked up on the profile.'

'Well done, you,' said Tony. 'Or rather, well done, me. Is the army missing a gunboat?'

'One was reported sunk during manoeuvres in Guantanamo a few months ago, but the wreckage was never recovered.'

'And now it turns up here, a hundred miles from an environmental summit in a riverside centre.'

'Maybe. Fifty percent, remember?'

'Can you get anything more on infrared?'

'Nope. Ran that already. Too cold.'

'Anyone on the island?'

'No hot bodies showing up, but I do see a craft moving down the coast on a rendezvous course. ETA thirty minutes.'

Tony Stark did not deliberate for long. 'Okay. Change of plan. I need to decommission that gunboat.'

Friday disagreed. 'No, boss, you don't. Call it in. Let the coast guard handle it.'

'The Irish Coast Guard is not armed,' said Tony. 'And even if it was, how far away is the nearest boat?'

Friday ran a quick scan of coast guard GPSs. 'An hour at best.'

'By which time whoever is heading for that gunboat will be locked and loaded.'

'And what about you, boss? You're locked and loaded with fireworks and disco music.'

Tony didn't need to listen to Friday's arguments, but sometimes it was good to bounce his impetuous thoughts off the voice of reason.

'Friday, let's do a quick recon. If it is the gunboat, I will pull out the spark plugs and leave her dead in the water. Then I call it in. No firepower necessary. If it isn't the boat, then we continue on to the party with no egg on our faceplate. Either way, it's a twenty-minute diversion. Okay?'

'Okay, boss,' said Friday, who knew that she wasn't really being asked. Tony Stark rarely passed up an opportunity for do-good adventuring.

In Tony Stark's considerable experience, the best tactic to employ in this kind of situation was the direct approach. More often than not, the mere sight of a grim-faced Iron Man descending from the sky like the hammer of justice was enough to send terrorists and bad guys scurrying, especially if they had seen YouTube footage of him smashing various weapons dumps and arms markets, which most of the world had. Often Tony would disengage the suit's mufflers and come in with every light blazing, whipping up more consternation than a troop carrier. But in this particular case, discretion was the wisest option, as there was a fifty-fifty chance that he would find nothing more sinister under the tarp than a trawler laid up for repairs.

A trawler laid up for repairs in the summer on an uninhabited island?

Okay, maybe that explanation didn't fly, but there were still a dozen reasons a boat could be hidden on an island that didn't include a raid on an environmental summit. In any case, there was no one on the island to stop him from taking a peek, so there was no need to wake the neighbours, even if they were only gulls.

A thought occurred to him. 'Friday, there are no ecological factors here, are there? I don't want to knock over an egg and cause the extinction of some breed of seabird. I have enough on my conscience as it is.'

'I think you're good, boss. You can always feed the chicks caviar in an emergency.'

'Hilarious. Remind me why I pay you, again?'

'You don't pay me, boss. Unless the currency is the sheer joy of your company.'

'Sarcasm now? You *are* evolving.'

Tony cupped his hands and brought his fingertips close together, powering down his magneto plasma thrusters so the suit descended smoothly to fifty feet above sea level.

'Run the full spectrum,' he instructed Friday. 'I want to know if there's anything bigger than a small dog on that island.'

On the helmet display he saw a laser grid draped over the island; thousands of red heartbeats popped up.

'Nothing but birds, bats and rodents, boss. No humans anywhere on the island.'

'What about surveillance?'

'Amazingly, we are in a dark zone. Not a single eye in the sky. Even that French satellite has moved on. It's not often you find a place like this.'

Tony frowned. 'It all seems too safe.'

'Imagine that. A safe reconnaissance with no one shooting at us. How frustrating!'

Tony ignored this additional example of Friday's

evolution. 'What kind of terrorist leaves a gunboat unguarded?'

'One who's on the way here right now. Boss, I hate to quote Hollywood, but I've got a bad feeling about this. If you absolutely must investigate, let's get it done before that boat gets any closer.'

'Can you see anything under the camouflage tarp?'

'No heartbeats, boss. But beyond that, nada. There might be a coating on the underside, or it might just be really old.'

Tony Stark did not like unknowns, but he knew that he had no choice but to investigate the craft. The boat was a mystery, and Tony's entire career was built on solving mysteries. He could no more walk away from this one than Captain America could pass a star-spangled banner without saluting.

'Okay,' he said. 'Down we go.'

He reduced thrust by fifteen percent, which took the suit out of hover mode and into a slow descent, with arms tight to the sides and hands and feet angled outward in a position that Friday referred to as "the penguin".

Tony supposed that it might look a little ungainly, but at least doing the penguin allowed him to observe on the way down.

'Ten seconds to touchdown, Friday,' he said.

To which the onboard AI said, 'I don't think so, boss.'

There was something in the way she said *boss*, a new sneer in the tone that Tony didn't care for. He was about to say something when things spiralled rapidly out of his control.

First, a flashing skull appeared on his display, accompanied by a deafening foghorn blast that threatened to burst Tony's eardrums.

'Friday!' he called, though he could not hear his own voice. 'Friday! Mute the speakers.'

The speakers did not mute; if anything, the volume increased, disorienting Tony completely. Initially, he blamed this disorientation for the sudden lurch in his stomach, the feeling that he was falling without control.

Then Tony thought, *Oh, crap. I* am *falling without control. Thrusters are not operational. What else can go wrong?*

The answer to that question was apparently: *Sensors. All of them.*

In addition to a crazy, deafening tumble, Tony Stark was suddenly completely blind.

Blind, deaf and tumbling.

Surely top three in the Never Do This During an Operation list.

He crashed into the tarpaulin and it wrapped about the armour like a net. Tony tried to thrash his way out, but the servomotors that allowed him to control the suit's limbs and digits were frozen. Tony had no choice but to lie as still as a statue while persons unknown, who were not supposed to be on the island, pounced on the Party Pack.

Inside the suit, Tony fought to regain some kind of control, but Friday was unresponsive and after a while he felt silly shouting 'Reboot!' at the flashing skull on his screen.

This is bad, he thought. *Extremely bad.*

And it was. There was no way to spin whatever was happening as possibly a good thing.

Whatever was happening was as follows: Iron Man crashed into the tarpaulin, which had been draped over what looked like a common-variety fishing craft and not the missing U.S. gunboat. Friday had predicted that the shape might very well not be a gunboat, but what she had not told Tony about were the two men who were exposed when the tarp was dragged into the boat's hold. These men were armed with conventional sharp implements and automatic weapons but also with compact electromagnets, which they lobbed onto the swathed Iron Man before trussing him in more layers of tarpaulin. They were aware that Iron Man's armour would not be affected by magnetic pull, but the electromagnetic fields would hamper any of his attempts to regain control of the suit.

Once the electromagnets were clustered on the prone Tony Stark, the two men efficiently folded any loose flaps of tarp over Iron Man. One of them, a giant of an individual, actually hummed the tune of Black Sabbath's "Iron Man" as he worked. Cole Vanger, known as Pyro to his associates in the ecoterrorism world because of the twin shoulder-mounted flamethrowers he was rarely without, didn't even realize he was doing it. Vanger also didn't realize the incredible irony of someone claiming to love the environment using flamethrowers as his weapons of choice. In truth, Vanger was not a genuine ecoterrorist; he just pretended to be because he thought radical women would appreciate it.

Once Stark was cocooned in tarpaulin, the next step was to wrap the package in duct tape, which is an incredibly strong material – not strong enough to restrain a functioning Iron Man but certainly of sufficient resilience to hold the package together for the brief but punishing journey on which it was about to embark. The second man was charged with the duct-taping, and he had been practising on Vanger for days. The unfortunate Pyro had spent hours with his limbs encased in plastic piping, thrashing weakly while his comrade trussed him up in tarp and tape. But this was not rehearsal; this was the real thing. And the man did his employer proud, mummifying Stark in under thirty seconds. Truly, the wielder of the tape was the duct-tape equivalent of a one-man Formula One pit crew.

'Allez!' cried the duct boss, who was a Frenchman named Freddie Leveque. *'Allez vite!'*

Leveque rapped three ringing knocks on an exposed inch of Iron Man's visor to emphasize just how *vite* they should *allez*.

The next step was to lasso Iron Man with a thick rope that snaked from the boat across the sloped slipway. The rope disappeared into the belly of a bush that was big enough to hide a truck. But it did not hide a truck; what it hid was a tractor with a thick rope tethered to its tow bar. The woman driving the tractor was known to Interpol by various names, including Valentina Zhuk, Valeria Zucchero, Vasha V8, the Zhukster, Zhuky, Tailspin and simply Spin, and she was accustomed to being behind the wheel of automobiles a whole lot faster than a tractor. Spin Zhuk was famous in certain nefarious circles for being the wheelwoman who won a grueling international rally race in a corporately sponsored experimental vehicle and then stole the vehicle.

At Leveque's signal, Spin Zhuk cranked the diesel engine, which she had personally stripped and tuned until it ran smoother than a ten-thousand-dollar Swiss watch, and floored the accelerator, hammering the big tractor through the bush and up the old fishing lane towards the medieval prison ruins at the crest of the hill. The Iron Man tape-'n'-tarp package was dragged ignominiously behind, over a plank laid across the fishing boat's gunwale, and bounced jerkily along the slipway, obeying Murphy's Law by bashing into every possible obstacle on the short journey. Vanger and Leveque swarmed behind like urchin children, crying *'Olé!'* and punching the air after each impact. For the most part the impacts were cushioned by the wrapping, but often a crag or sharp corner of a brick penetrated the uneven cocoon, and the curve and purity of the metal made a bong ring across the small island.

'Ding-dong,' called Cole Vanger. 'Iron Man is dead!'

This was not strictly true, but it won him a laugh from the other man, and heaven knew there would be precious few laughs in the days ahead.

Spin Zhuk put the pedal to the metal as much as a person could in a Massey Ferguson tractor and swore in Ukrainian as the farm vehicle spluttered its way up the steep approach to the prison.

'You are a stupid metal pig,' she told the tractor. 'My grandfather runs faster than you, and he died fighting the Russians.'

There were other words, too, more offensive even than *stupid* or *pig*, and if the tractor had been capable of taking offence, it might have considered stalling for a moment, before deciding that maybe it would try to squeeze out a little extra horsepower to avoid even more insults. In any event, sentient or no, the vehicle bucked and seemed to attack the incline with new vigour.

The macabre parade snaked up the rocky trail to the medieval ruins, with Leveque easily outpacing the other man, using the almost incredible obstacle-course skills he had picked up in the French Foreign Legion. Leveque scaled the outer wall and winched open a camouflage net that hung across a granite arch. The arch had once supported a studded door and portcullis, but it had since crumbled and now sagged like the mouth of a mournful giant. If this operation were being run according to union rules, then health and safety would surely have vetoed access through the leaning arch, but these particular soldiers were not members of any union, and it was pretty much taken for granted that their health and safety would be at risk during every second of the operation. As if to highlight this point, the arch collapsed completely due to the vibration of the heavy vehicle's passage, burying the Iron Man package in rubble. Spin Zhuk swore as the tractor jerked to a halt, then steered from left to right in a tight fan, wiggling Iron Man out from under the fallen stone. Freddie Leveque escaped injury by executing a neat sideways tumble, which drew another *'Olé!'* from Cole Vanger.

Once the package was free, Spin proceeded along the planned route, driving the tractor through a doorway they had widened earlier and down a braced wooden ramp, directly into the heart of the old prison. The jail had once housed hundreds of pirates, murderers, swindlers, smugglers and political prisoners, but it was now to be home to a single very special detainee. Down there the ceilings were low and oppressive, the air was dank and foul, and the huffing generator and banks of computer screens seemed thoroughly out of place.

A portly Asian man with hair and beard clipped to a uniform tennis ball length spun on his office chair to face the tractor that had just thundered into the subterranean chamber, literally shaking the foundations. With an expression of mild surprise on his face, like *Oh, is it that time already?* he clapped three times.

'Excellent, Miss Zhuk,' he said. 'Wonderful, in fact. Let's take a look, shall we, gentlemen?'

Vanger and Leveque trotted down the ramp and set to work with diverse blades, quickly stripping back the layers of tarpaulin to reveal the world-famous red-and-gold Iron Man armour, semi-submerged in electromagnets like a toy at the bottom of a cereal box.

The bearded man, who was known to his men simply as chef – in the *boss* sense of the word, not the *cook* sense – flexed his fingers like a concert pianist and turned back to his computer.

'Now, time to say hello to Mr Stark.'

'No!' came a distant voice, accompanied by rapid footsteps down the spiral staircase that led into the chamber from the battlements. 'Wait.'

But the chef had not heard or would not wait. He tapped a line of code into his keyboard and the Iron Man armour peeled away from Tony Stark, leaving him as defenceless as a clam without its shell.

Almost.

Inside the suit, Tony had quickly realized that there was nothing for him to do but ride out the concussive trip. The suit's assorted shock absorbers, gyros and dampeners spared him a good portion of the impact, but he was still battered and bruised by the time the suit came to rest.

The foghorn faded in his earpieces, which was a blessed relief, and gave Tony a moment to gather his thoughts as he heard the first telltale *clink* that signaled the impending removal of the Iron Man suit.

Luckily, Tony Stark was a bona fide genius and could gather more thoughts in a moment than most people could assemble in one lifetime and several reincarnations.

His lightning assessment of the situation was as follows:

The suit has been somehow compromised, but no serious attempt has been made to damage it, which means that whoever is behind this wants it intact. Or perhaps they want me *intact. Worst-case scenario: they want the suit alive but billionaire playboy dead. Unlikely. A rich genius is always more valuable alive than six feet under. So I have been lured here by someone who somehow stymied all my systems and therefore knows them intimately. Which narrows down the list of possible suspects considerably.*

Actually, I am the only suspect on the list.

Was I manipulated somehow?

Was I drugged? Hypnotized?

Perhaps none of this is even happening, though it's probably best to proceed under the assumption that it is, because this suit is about to open and when it does there will be people waiting to, at the very least, make me do things I don't want to do.

Conclusion: this is not going to be as much fun as Graywolf's party.

Course of action: do not go down without a fight.

Tony Stark's startle reflex had always been somewhat

exaggerated, or as Nick Fury had once put it: 'Stark, you are jumpier than a sack of guilt.' Never one to ignore a potential asset, Stark had worked on this one through meditation and training until he could act with the speed of a reflexive reaction. Simply put: when Tony Stark felt the need for speed, he could move as though someone had stuck a pin in his behind.

And Tony Stark felt that particular need right now.

When the Iron Man armour folded, slotted and whirred back, Stark's captors were expecting to find a dazed industrialist who was soft and useless without his space-age armour. What they certainly were not expecting was a highly trained and motivated individual who flew out of the suit as though ejected.

Cole Vanger stood closest to the "package" and had the smug grin wiped off his face when Tony Stark did not plead for his life but instead seemed to analyze Vanger's armaments while flying towards him, preparing to turn them to his own advantage.

'What?' said Vanger, and then, 'Huh?'

Then Stark's head-butt had broken his nose and the industrialist's thumbs were covering Vanger's.

Don't do that, Vanger might have said if pain had not filled his skull, displacing any rational thought. *You'll ignite my flamethrowers.*

This, of course, was exactly what Tony Stark had in mind. Vanger's flamethrower nozzles were mounted on his shoulders like the robotic parrots of a techno pirate, and at this angle they were pointed directly into the exposed guts of the Iron Man rig. Tony reasoned that if he couldn't use the suit, then no one should be able to. All depended on the kind of fuel this guy had. Old-fashioned kerosene wouldn't do much more than heat the plates a few degrees and maybe buckle a couple of them, but if he had something a little more gel-based in the tanks, then that could be it for the Party Pack.

Tony pressed down on Vanger's thumbs and then drew the man close, as if they were doing the rhumba. They were not dancing; it was simply that Tony had no desire to get his ears burned off by the jets of flame shooting over both shoulders.

As it turned out, it didn't matter what kind of fuel Cole "Pyro" Vanger was packing, because the flames had barely licked the suit's innards when Freddie Leveque crashed into the pair, sending the jumble of limbs and trunks rolling across the chamber, which had positive and negative results for both sides.

From Tony's point of view, it was a darn shame that the flames did not get a chance to damage the suit, as, like any inventor, he hated to give away tech. On the other hand, the flaming arc that continued to spurt from Vanger's flamethrowers did some considerable damage to his kidnappers' equipment, frying two monitors entirely and sending the remaining men scurrying for cover.

'Restrain him!' cried the chef, irritated. 'What do I

pay you *báichī* for?'

Tony held on to his presence of mind and located Leveque's head, which was jammed into Vanger's armpit. Fortunately, Tony's foot was also in that vicinity, so he clipped Leveque's forehead with the sole of one sneaker, wishing that he had opted to wear his hard leather loafers instead.

And people say fashion isn't important, he thought, scrambling over the stunned Leveque and assessing the building as he ran.

One obvious exit along the ramp … There may be more men up there … They probably have orders not to kill me, but still, they might be a little disconcerted by the pyrotechnics …

In Tony's experience, disconcerted triggermen tended to be a little happy on their triggers. So he discounted the ramp option almost immediately and veered left toward the shadows.

Be a stairwell, he broadcast at the shadows. *Be a stairwell.*

And a stairwell there miraculously was. It was virtually unguarded, too, aside from the echoing smacks of footsteps descending from above, but Tony was already committed to that direction.

I would rather take my chances with mystery footsteps than a room full of bullets, flames and angry men, Tony decided.

So upwards it was. Tony raced up the spiral staircase two steps at a time, slipping more than once on the slick stone. Whoever was coming was coming down fast, and Tony decided he would take a breath and use the momentum of the mystery descender against him.

So he stopped suddenly and ducked, figuring the man would go tumbling over his hunched form. But just as suddenly, the footsteps halted, as though the hidden person had caught on to his plan.

There was no time for delay, as the other men had gathered themselves and were hustling in his direction; so Tony, having quickly considered his options, decided to keep going.

Stay down, he told himself. *Never be where you're supposed to be.*

On he went, rounding the corner at high speed, ready to roll the man across his back, sending him crashing into his comrades like a human bowling ball. That would surely buy Tony a few more seconds to figure a way out of this ruin.

But no one went tumbling over Tony Stark's dipped shoulders. Instead, Tony came nose to toe with a pair of green-laced, scuffed army boots. A bemused voice floated down to him.

'Never be where you're supposed to be, right?'

Tony looked up to see green eyes gazing down at him, framed by a mop of red curly hair.

'Hello, boss,' said the girl.

Tony knew that voice well. It travelled with him everywhere.

'You sound like Friday,' said Tony. He rapped experimentally on the steel toe cap of one boot. 'But you're real. I don't understand.'

'Wow,' said Friday. 'Tony Stark doesn't understand. I should take a photo.'

And then she shot him in the neck with a trank so big that Tony was knocked immediately back to the 1980s.

'Duran Duran, Dad,' he mumbled. 'They're a band. Hello.'

He keeled over backwards, tumbling down the stairs he had so craftily raced up.

Not craftily enough, it turned out.

The last thing Tony felt before he passed out was puzzlement, and that would be the first thing he felt when he woke up.

Well, technically the second thing. The first would be pain.

THAT FRIDAY FEELING

If Tony Stark had been offered the choice of waking up or staying down in the shadows for a while, he would absolutely have picked the latter. Stark had been knocked senseless enough times to know that the *waking up* part was always a rough ride, especially when the cocktail of trauma and drugs that had put him out in the first place was extreme.

His buddy Rhodey had said once, 'You know, Tony man, every time you take a hit, you lose a few IQ points. Keep this up and soon you won't be a genius no more.'

To which Tony had said, 'You mean soon I won't be a genius *any*more, genius.'

And then Rhodey had gotten offended and they'd ended up wrestling in the den and putting a hole in a

P. J. Lynch oil painting that was worth more than a top-of-the-line sports car.

Tony felt his consciousness bloom inside the darkness of his head now, and with the bloom came three kinds of pain: sharp, dull and aching.

What's happening? he thought. *Oh my god. My head is exploding.*

The puzzlement persisted all the way into consciousness, and Stark found himself wedged under a bunk bed in the corner of a windowless room with moss-covered stone walls and a barred door.

Outside the door sat Friday, on a blue plastic chair that must have come from a kindergarten classroom somewhere. She was dressed in rainbow leggings and army boots, and her red curls fizzed over the collar of an oversize combat jacket.

'Do you like your cell?' she asked.

Tony presumed this was rhetorical and did not answer, deciding to use his energy to crawl out from under the bunk.

'Really, Friday?' he said at last, in between gasps of air. 'You had to stash me under the bed like some kind of troll?'

'You put yourself under the bed, boss,' retorted Friday. 'I'd have a shrink look into that. I know the S.H.I.E.L.D. psychiatrist has been dying to get you in a padded cell for years. But I asked you about *this* cell. Maybe you don't like it, but you should appreciate its design. The classic prison cell. Basically unchanged for centuries. Four walls and a door. In functional terms, this room is like the spoon. It can't be improved upon.'

Tony rolled onto his back. 'I've been in prison cells before, Friday. Maybe you heard?'

'Afghanistan?' said Friday. 'I did hear. The whole world heard. A billionaire is imprisoned for a month and the entire planet goes crazy. But this time is different.'

'Yeah, how so?'

'Why don't you tell me, genius?'

Tony sat up, scratching the bristles of his laser-cut goatee. 'How is this incarceration different? Let me see. I would guess you have learned from the mistakes of my last captors, so you won't be asking me to build anything dangerous.'

'Correct,' Friday confirmed. 'We already have what we need from you.'

'The suit, I suppose.'

'Suppose what you will.'

'And you'll keep me isolated?' Tony guessed.

'Right again. No chance for any mind games.'

Tony wiggled his fingers in the style of Doctor Strange. 'Yeah? Maybe I'm playing a mind game right now.'

'I've been inside your mind, remember? None of your clever manipulations will work on me.'

'Unless they're already working.'

'Now you're being childish.'

'Now *you're* being childish.'

Friday sighed. 'You don't get it, do you? You've got nothing. Every stitch of clothing has been removed. We wanded your hair and bones. They even yanked out that crown on your molar in case there was a tracker in there.'

Tony noticed that he was wearing a black sweat suit with gold stripes down the arms and legs.

'This is actually quite cool – in a retro kind of way. Can I keep it?'

'Of all the things you could ask me, that's what you pick? What's the matter, Tony? Too insecure to admit that you're baffled?'

This struck home, but Tony did not allow so much as a flicker of that insecurity to show on his face.

'Friday – if that's your name, which I'm guessing it's not, since you're real now and all. Flesh and bone, as it were. Tell me, does your mother know that you run around in the evenings kidnapping billionaires?'

Friday stood, a bored expression settling on her face. 'Okay, boss, if that's the way it's going to be. I would have liked you to understand what's happening here, because it's important to me, but this mission is time sensitive, so if you want to fool around doing the whole Tony Stark thing, I'll see you later.' She flicked a sarcastic salute at the man who was obviously not her boss anymore and headed for the stone steps.

Tony had participated in enough high-powered boardroom strategizing to recognize a bluff when he heard it. Friday was just dying to tell him what was happening, so he pulled himself to his feet and gave her an incendiary remark to drag it out of her.

'You won't see me later, Friday. You'll see me *sooner*. And I might have to dock your pay.'

Friday spun on her heel. 'You are such a dimwit in so many ways. You've been outplayed, Stark. Accept it.'

'Is that what this is all about? Outplaying me? Seems like a lot of effort. So all I gotta do is say I give in and we'll call it a day?'

'No!' said Friday. 'It never had to go this far. I gave you your chance, remember?'

There was fire in the girl's eyes, and Tony got the feeling that he had somehow driven her crazy, which wouldn't be the first time he had done that to a person. But this one was just a teen.

'I don't know you, kid. We've never met.'

This riled Friday even more. '*We've never met?* We've never met? The two of us haven't encountered each other before?'

Tony was genuinely mystified. 'You're just asking the same question different ways. Have we met, or haven't we?'

'I gave you a way out of this,' said Friday, eyes wide. 'I put the file in your manicured hands. Port Verdé? Ring any bells in that big vain head?'

Tony saw an opening. 'Do you mean big-*veined* head? That's because my brain needs more than the average blood supply. It's a by-product of being a genius.' Then he stopped being what only he considered funny and his face dropped.

'Port Verdé. Oh.'

'Yes,' said Friday. 'That's right, buddy. *Oh.*'

'The orphanage. I remember now. Then you must be ...'

Friday slow-clapped. 'The intern. And finally, the penny drops. The mist clears. The genius takes his head out of his –'

'That situation is not my fault. I had nothing to do with that,' Tony objected.

'You sure didn't,' said Friday. 'Port Verdé might as well have been another dimension as far as Tony Stark was concerned. After all, what are twenty orphan girls and an aid worker in the grand scheme of things?'

Tony was done joking now. Port Verdé had been a tough choice, the kind that kept him awake at night.

'That's not fair, kid. I gave that request serious consideration. I even talked to S.H.I.E.L.D. but Nick Fury threw me out of his office.' Even as he said it, Tony knew that Friday would see that excuse for the crock of lameness it was.

'Oh, sure,' said Friday in a voice that could not have been frostier if she had been wearing ice boots and sitting at the South Pole. 'Nick Fury said no. And when Nicky says "Jump," Tony says, "How high?" That's a load of horse dung, *boss*. You've been running solo ops for months. I planned some of them. But only to clear up the Stark mess, never to help people out – other than yourself, obviously.'

'It's more complicated than that,' objected Tony. 'There is a very delicate political balance in Fourni. Iron Man can't just go barging in there waving the stars and stripes. The new president is doing everything he can to stabilize the country, and I have to give him a chance to do that.'

'My sister can't wait for the country to stabilize, so Iron Man *will* be going to Port Verdé to kick a gang out of an orphanage and rescue my sister. Only this time Tony Stark won't be behind the wheel, because he'd rather go to a pop star's party.'

'Rock star,' Tony said absently, because something else had occurred to him. 'Never call Wolf a pop star. He starts howling at the moon.'

Friday was almost dumbstruck. 'Are you even listening to me? Do you even know what's going on here?'

Tony snapped back on. 'Okay, Friday. That's not your real name, I know, but I can't remember that right now, so don't get all offended.'

'It's Saoirse Tory,' said the girl who had been Friday. '*Seer-sha*. In Irish it means *freedom*, which my sister doesn't presently have. But soon she will, thanks to your suit.'

Tony gripped the bars. 'Seer-sha, right. I remember now. Listen, Saoirse, these people, the men … they found you, right? Not the other way around.'

'Wrong!' said Saoirse. 'I found *them*. I knew that I

couldn't do this alone. So I recruited a team.'

'You recruited them on your own?' Tony persisted. 'Think, kid. This is important.'

'If you must know, *boss*, I recruited Mr Chen, who, unlike you, is a real philanthropist. He used his contacts to sign up the other three members of our team.'

Tony felt sick to his stomach. For a moment he had hoped that all this was simply a kid trying to take international law into her own hands, but it suddenly became all too clear that there were shadowy forces at work.

'Saoirse, listen to me. These guys, they don't care about your sister. There's an environmental summit eighty miles from here. You know that. Do you think that's a coincidence?'

Saoirse smirked. 'Mr Chen said that you would try to sow doubt in my mind. We had to get you over here, and that was the best way. I volunteered you for the gig.'

'I thought the Irish president invited me.'

Saoirse's smirk graduated to a full-grown smile. 'Yep, that's what you *thought*. In fact, the president accepted your kind offer, boss.'

Tony returned the smirk. 'When you say *boss*, it feels like you mean something else entirely.'

'I always did,' said Saoirse.

'Are you a hundred percent sure the summit diversion was your idea?'

Saoirse thought about it. 'Mr Chen may have been the

one who mentioned it, but I was the one who followed through. I hijacked your system and set the whole thing up. Nothing works without me.'

'Nothing up to this point,' said Tony. 'Which was why they needed you.'

'They need me because I *am* the plan. Listen, *boss*, I am not falling for your mind games, so why don't you give it a rest?'

Tony pushed his face as far through the bars as possible, giving himself a temporary face-lift. 'Kid, I'm begging you. Let me out of here right now. If you don't, we're both dead. And that's just for starters. This Chen guy is not who he says he is.'

'I know *exactly* who Mr Chen is,' said Saoirse, with a cocky expression Tony recognized from countless photos of himself. 'I ran background on him times infinity, okay? I know computers, Tony. Look what I did to the famous Stark OS.'

'You may know computers, kid, but you don't know people.'

'Ha!' said Saoirse. 'I don't know people? Me? You had a *person* in your ear for the last few months and *you* thought it was a robot. And let me tell you, I am so glad to be out of your head. Because I have met some jerks in my time, but you are king of that hill. You are the top of that heap. Manicures and facials. I never met anyone so shallow.'

'That is quite possibly true,' admitted Tony, 'but it is not the point right now, kid. The point at this moment is that you have hacked a very dangerous weapon on the eve of an environmental summit that could change the world.'

'Dangerous weapon, sure,' said Saoirse, pooh-poohing the idea. 'It's the Party Pack. In forty-eight hours it will be expensive junk.'

'You can do a lot of damage in forty-eight hours,' said Tony.

'I won't be doing any damage,' countered Friday. 'I am simply going to drop into an orphanage, clean out the rats, and scoop up my sister.'

Tony might have gotten through to Saoirse had two figures not trotted down the ramp into the dungeon area. One was Flamethrower Guy, and the other was a harmless-looking bespectacled gent with neat hair and beard. This, Tony presumed, was the philanthropist Chen.

'Miss Tory, we are having some problems with the right gauntlet,' he said, his accent faintly Chinese. 'It will not activate.'

Saoirse frowned. 'It should work fine; there was no systems damage.'

Tony barked a laugh. 'Uh-huh. No systems damage. Why would there be? All you did was cover me in magnets and drag me across an island.'

'Can you fix it?' asked Chen calmly.

'It isn't broken,' Saoirse insisted. 'Stark's up to something.'

Chen seemed unperturbed. 'Can you fix it?'

Saoirse talked really slow. 'Mr Chen, this is space-age

engineering. We're in a medieval castle. No one can fix it here, but like I said, it isn't broken.'

Vanger moved close to Chen and whispered in his ear, all the while staring murderously at Stark.

'Nice nose job you got there, sparky,' said Tony. 'Bet that stings a little, huh?'

Cole Vanger balled his fists and stepped forward, but Chen halted him with the merest dip of his chin.

'Can you do it without Stark's gauntlet, Mr Vanger?' asked Chen.

Vanger nodded, the fury never leaving his eyes, and Tony predicted that when kill-Tony-time came, as he was certain it would, this guy would be at the front of the volunteer line, priming his flamethrowers.

'Yeah, I can do it, chef,' he said to Chen. 'You bet I can. I got my own helmet and my own gauntlet. My gauntlet's better, as a matter of fact. All this does is save us time.'

Saoirse was a little puzzled. 'Do what? What are you talking about, Cole?'

Chen was placating. 'Nothing, dear child. Just small operational details.'

But Saoirse had picked up on the mood change. 'What's going on, Mr Chen? Cole doesn't need a gauntlet. I'm the one who'll be flying the suit.'

Chen steepled his fingers. 'As I said, child, small operational details.'

Stark stuck his oar in. 'Come on, guy, why don't you

fess up? Tell the kid how dumb she's been.'

Chen smiled. 'Dumb? This child has been dumb? She cyberstalked you for months. She brought the Iron Man package halfway across the world and rendered it inoperable. She did with a laptop and headset what every hacker in the world has been attempting for years. And she is, as you say, *dumb*? If that is so, then you are dumb squared.'

'Dumb squared,' said Tony. 'Math jokes. Cute.'

Chen's smile grew a few white teeth wider. 'Jokes, yes, I am most happy. You are about to make me a lot of money, Mr Tony Stark.'

Saoirse's balloon was deflating and whistling as it fell. 'Money? What are you talking about, Mr Chen?'

Chen's smile was replaced with an irritated frown. 'Be quiet, you buzzing bee of a child. The adults are talking now. Our little charade is over.'

Most teens probably would have kept spouting questions, but Saoirse Tory knew enough to realize that more information would not lead to increased happiness. In fact, she suspected that the more she knew about how she had been duped, the more of a duped dope she would feel.

So she ran, dodging Cole Vanger's grabbing fingers but unfortunately heading straight into the arms of Spin Zhuk, who had just walked onto the ramp.

Spin stashed Saoirse under one arm, ignoring the teenager's struggles.

'I am guessing that the jig is, as they say, up, no?'

'Yes, indeed,' said Chen.

'Whatever you're planning,' shouted Saoirse, 'it won't work without me, Chen.'

Chen sighed and unbuttoned his shirt. Underneath he wore a vest of molded padding, which had lent him his portly aspect.

'This is Chen,' he said, undoing the Velcro straps and stripping off the fat suit. 'Helpful, comforting Chen. Chen, who is concerned for orphans in Port Verdé. Chen the philanthropist, who allowed himself to be located by clever Saoirse Tory. Chen, who will do anything to help poor Saoirse Tory recover her sister. Chen, who is prepared to bankroll a mercy mission. That is Chen.'

Chen seemed to stand taller than he had before, and his muscular chest was adorned with an intricate dragon tattoo.

'Do not refer to me as Chen from this moment on.' From his pockets, the man formerly known as Chen took ten rings and placed them on specific fingers.

'Here it comes,' said Tony.

The man who had been Chen glared at Saoirse with intense green eyes.

'From this moment on,' he said, 'you may call me the Mandarin.'

'Crud,' swore Tony, sliding to the floor of his cell. 'We are toast.'

GAME THEORY

What's the story, Saoirse Tory?

This rhyming question had followed Saoirse around school since she was five years old. Thanks to her grandfather's home tutoring on their private island, the precocious young Saoirse was already able to read by the time she landed in Kilmore school from Little Saltee, which earned her a reputation as a bit of a M.O.D.O.K. (Mental Organism Designed Only for Killing). Her teacher took to asking her, 'What's the story, Saoirse Tory?' whenever her classmates from the mainland were unable to answer a question, which was often. If it had not been the young teacher's first year out of college, she might have anticipated that the other students would turn her affectionate rhyme into a taunt.

'What's the story, Saoirse Tory?' became a stick to beat Saoirse with whenever she volunteered an answer or even corrected a teacher.

Thus it was unfortunate that Tony Stark happened upon the rhyme as they sat side by side on the cell floor – both now prisoners.

'So, kid. Saoirse Tory, right? Well, tell me: what's the story, Saoirse Tory?'

Saoirse groaned. 'I never heard that one before.'

'Hey, I'm a little off my game, okay? Some know-it-all teen got conned by the most notorious assassin-terrorist type on the planet, and here I am in a cell.'

'You got conned first, *boss*,' Saoirse retorted.

Tony disagreed. 'Technically, you were conned first, if you think about it.'

'Let's say we both got conned. One of us has to be mature.'

'Whatever, stupid face,' said Tony maturely.

They sat in silence for a few minutes, both turning their not inconsiderable brains to the problem of being incarcerated by a notorious murderer. When Saoirse couldn't figure an immediate way out, she turned to Stark.

'Go on, ask me,' she said.

'Ask you what?'

'You know what. You're dying to.'

Tony *was* dying to, so he did. 'Okay, kid. Lay it out for me. How did you do it? People have been trying to jailbreak the Iron Man system for years. It's a constant thing. I've had entire government sections devoted to just that, and some Irish teenager manages it from an ancient ruin on an island. I can't believe you're that smart, so how did you do it?'

Saoirse had been dying to tell just as much as Tony had been dying to ask, so she said, 'First, I am *that* smart, smart enough to build my own operations centre on the island. And second, I used something called game theory. Did you ever hear of that, boss?'

'Sure,' said Tony. 'Game theory. The study of strategic decision making. John Nash. Won the Nobel Prize, right?'

'That's him. Well, I expanded on his theories.'

'You expanded on John Nash?'

'It wasn't hard. Anyway, in simple terms –'

'Thanks, I appreciate it.'

'To make it simple, to solve an equation or problem, sometimes you need to go after the elements that are not yet in play and wait.'

Tony actually slapped his forehead. 'Of course! You went directly after Friday.'

'I had to intern for a month and do a hell of a lot of snooping, but eventually I found out that the artificial intelligences were stored in your own private lab.'

'So you came by one evening.'

'That night I came over with the Port Verdé proposal. Remember how upset I was when you turned me down?'

'I do. Girls always cry around me; I don't know what it is.'

'Yeah, boohoo. I was so devastated I had to use your bathroom.'

'By the lab,' said Tony.

'Yeah, the specs to your house are online, you know. Your security system is pretty basic. So I froze the cameras, turned up the heat to fox the thermals, and spiked the Friday disk, which was, believe it or not, lying on top of your desk.'

Tony winced. 'Right on the desk, huh? That seems a little careless in hindsight.'

He recalled the night now, some months previous – an unusually wet night for California, with low barrelling clouds rumbling across the Pacific's surface. Tony had been about to turn in when the high school intern from Stark showed up at his gate begging for ten minutes of his time. So he let her in and she laid out this plan she had for Iron Man to fly down to Fourni's Port Verdé and eject a pirate gang from a girls orphanage on the city limits. And while he was there, perhaps he could also rescue her sister.

It was a heartbreaking situation but one in which Tony Stark couldn't interfere right then; the new president was making real strides in Fourni, and it would not do for Iron Man to upset the apple cart before the leader could carry out his own plan. So he had gently turned the intern down and called an Uber to take her home. The poor thing had been utterly distraught and sobbed her little heart out in the basement restroom.

Yeah, fake sobbed while spiking my disk.

'You were convincing, I'll give you that, kid,' he said now. 'Crying your eyes out.'

'That wasn't *all* fake,' said Saoirse. 'My sister was a prisoner. She still is.'

'So you came back home and waited for me to plug Friday into the suit.'

'Exactly. But you were really plugging *me* in. And you never suspected a thing. Tony Stark actually thought the Friday program was evolving, which is pretty ridiculous, considering how crude it is. I actually made quite a few improvements.'

'Don't give yourself too much credit, kid,' said Tony, wounded a little by the *crude* jab. 'You were still taken in by the Mandarin and his merry men.'

'Yeah,' admitted Saoirse. 'I guess I feel just about as stupid as you must. I let Liz down, I let Granddad down and I suppose I delivered Iron Man into the wrong hands.'

Tony chuckled. 'You're being too easy on yourself, Saoirse. You *definitely* delivered Iron Man into the wrong hands, no *supposing* about it. You've heard of the Mandarin, right? The most infamous terrorist operating today. He's had his finger in almost every explosive pie of the last twenty years. He doesn't care about collateral damage. In fact, the more bodies the merrier. I've been on his trail for a decade. I came close a couple of times, but he gave me the slip.'

'I just wanted to save my sister,' said Saoirse. 'My intentions were good.'

'Said every misguided sap ever.'

'That's rich coming from you, sap.'

The conversation petered out at this point as both occupants of the cell realized the futility of continuing to insult each other. The real issue was the pickle they were in, and thinking of it as a *pickle* seemed a little optimistic. It was more like a crucible of terror and deadly danger, and it seemed unlikely that either prisoner would escape unscathed. And not only that, but it seemed pretty obvious that others would die.

The mood was made literally darker as the lights in their basement prison went out, leaving only the eerie glow of security monitors flickering on the walls. Tony must have nodded off for a while, so when Saoirse began speaking softly, it seemed almost as though she was communicating directly into his dreams.

'Granddad raised us both. Me and Liz. Everyone else left the island but we three. My granddad was special. You would have liked him I think, boss. A show-off, just like you. The Ancient Mariner, we called him. But Francis was his real name. Francis Tory. He had plans for this island; it was going to be an ecological utopia. Wind and wave power. Totally self-sustaining. Such grand plans. We grew up believing in those plans. After a few years the school couldn't keep up, so Granddad homeschooled us. He showed us how privileged we were to live here, and how it was our duty to help those less fortunate. I raised money for the Port Verdé Girls Home, but that wasn't enough for

Liz. She's a real hero, boss, if you ever want to meet one. No metal suit, no magic hammer. Just a degree in nursing and a bag of inoculations. She went down to Fourni with the Red Cross and looked after those girls. I raised the money, and she made sure every cent was spent wisely.'

Tony kept his eyes closed. 'But then?' he asked. There would have to be a 'but then.' In these stories there always was.

Saoirse did not answer for a long moment, but Tony thought he heard a snuffle and it reminded him that behind the bluster and smarts, Saoirse Tory was still a child.

'But then ...' she said. 'But then everything went wrong. A local gang took over the orphanage and kept Liz as their private nurse. Granddad and I tried every official channel to get her out, but he was old and the strain was too much for his poor heart. He died a year ago, and I knew that if I was put in the foster system I would never be able to help Liz. So I buried Francis Tory in his beloved vegetable patch and built a digital avatar of him to convince the mainland he was still alive.'

'And that's what gave you the idea to hijack my AI.'

'Yes. I thought I would appeal to your humanity first, but you turned me down. I was desperate.'

Tony was finding it difficult to stay annoyed at Saoirse Tory, even though she had most likely doomed them both. The kid was whip smart and had initiative coming out her ears. Also she could sling a good insult, which was something he had always appreciated.

He sat up and looked Saoirse squarely in the eyes. 'Okay, kid. We've all got family problems. What I need for you to do is bury that stuff deep down inside and let it fester for the time being. That's gotta be healthy, right?'

'How's that working for you, daddy's boy?'

'Pretty good. I'm a billionaire playboy philanthropist and so on. But listen, soon this Mandarin guy is gonna realize that it's not a great idea to incarcerate two brains like ourselves in the same room, so he's gonna wander in here, do a little gloating, then probably drag me out. You, they're going to keep alive until the mission is over.' Tony shifted, taking Saoirse by the shoulders. 'Whatever happens, don't break. They will tell you I'm dead, but don't believe it. Tony Stark has a few tricks up his sleeve. My daddy, who I have all the issues with, once told me to play my cards close to my chest. "Never tell them your secrets," he said. So I've got some stuff going on that not even Friday knows about, understand?'

Saoirse nodded. 'You're not dead,' she said.

'That's right, and neither are you. We fight till the end. We use our massive brains. This is your island, remember, so if you get loose, they will never find you.'

'That's right, they won't.'

'Find a way to contact me so I can come and rescue you.'

'Or I can come and rescue you.'

Tony almost said, 'Yeah, sure, because you've been such a great rescuer so far,' but he thought that was a bit close to the bone, so he pulled it back to, 'Yeah, sure. In your dreams.'

Saoirse must have read the thought on his face, because she flinched as though struck and pulled away, then retreated into the corner of the cell and curled up like a wounded animal.

The Mandarin made his appearance at first light with Leveque in tow, and as Tony had predicted, the *chef* was in a mood to gloat.

'Good morning to you both. The day has come when I, the Mandarin, shall secure my reputation as the greatest agent of chaos the world has ever seen.'

Tony rubbed his eyes. 'No eggs this morning, young man. Just a pot of black coffee. It's been a rough night.'

The Mandarin paced in front of the cell like a general addressing his troops. 'No, Stark. You cannot trump reality with your puerile American banter. In fact, if you interrupt again, I will have Freddie tase the child.'

Leveque bristled with barely restrained sadism. Here was a guy who would step on a puppy, and Tony noticed that he wore the Iron Man gauntlet.

'Per'aps I shock ze kid anyway,' he said.

The Mandarin affected a pained expression. 'Please, Monsieur Leveque. We do not shock children unless it is necessary.'

Tony positioned himself between Leveque and Saoirse, as if that would save the girl.

'You're going after the environmental ministers, right, Mandarin? That's the play?'

The Mandarin clapped his hands. 'Yes, of course that is *the play*. Mr Vanger will fly right into that convention centre and burn the place to the ground with his precious flamethrowers. We have replaced your gauntlet with one of his own, and the helmet is of our design, given the extraordinary size of Mr Vanger's skull. But we anticipated that.'

'You'll never make it past the security sweeps,' said Tony. 'They'll shoot him out of the sky.'

'I think not,' said the Mandarin smugly. 'All the protocols are stored onboard and, fortunately, Miss Tory unlocked your securities.'

Tony wished he had some way to puncture the Mandarin's smug bubble, but for now it looked as though the terrorist held all the cards. The Convention Centre Dublin would run a few scans on a suit that was a couple of decades ahead of its equipment and then welcome Iron Man with open barricades and safeties on.

'The real genius of this plan is the payment I receive,' continued the Mandarin. 'Which is not financial. No, my reward will be far more reaching than mere money.'

'Power,' guessed Tony.

'Exactly,' said the Mandarin. 'I have assembled evidence on each and every individual who has ever engaged my services. When this mission is complete, I will virtually own the new environmental ministers of several countries. I, the Mandarin, will control the fate of the world's environment and which companies are contracted to clean it up.'

'World domination through sewage,' said Tony. 'That's a new one.'

The Mandarin took the sarcasm as a compliment. 'And that is not the only novel facet to my plan. I have subverted the normal engagement protocols for common assassins in that I manufactured the targets. It's a business lesson I learned from your father. He was quoted in *Time* magazine as saying: "Sometimes the opportunity does not exist, and so you must create the opportunity." '

Tony remembered the quote. It had been one of his father's regulars, along with: 'We are Starks, Titans of the modern world,' and 'What the heck are you wearing, Tony?'

'You manufactured the targets?'

'Exactly,' said the Mandarin. 'Once I had decided who to eliminate, I wondered who would want me to kill them. And believe me, Mr Tony Stark, environmental ministers have many enemies. My little group will be owed favours from two motor companies, a logging multinational, a pharmacy giant, rival politicians – oh, and two angry spouses – to name but a few. One particular minister, the Swedish one I believe, has three bounties on his head. Such a naughty boy. Each client believes he is the only one. It is, as you Americans would say, *quite the sweet deal*. And all the blame will fall at your door, Mr Stark.'

'Not that I'll be alive to shoulder it,' guessed Tony.

The Mandarin wagged his finger, and Tony saw that his college ring glittered among the Mandarin's own ten rings. 'Precisely,' said the terrorist. 'Dead men deny nothing.'

Which is never a good thing to hear when the terrorist's finger is pointed in your direction.

5

A GENIUS AND AN IDIOT

The Mandarin had Tony dragged outside to the courtyard, cuffed hands jerked cruelly high behind his back. The sun was peeping through the crags of the western island, and the screeching gulls in morning flight were knife slashes in the sky. It was difficult for Tony to believe that so much had happened in a single night, and yet the world looked the same this morning.

The Mandarin stood in the centre of the flagstones, stripped to the waist, performing what looked like a combination of tai chi and disco dancing, which Tony, given his impulsive and foolhardy nature, could not help commenting on even though he could guess what it would cost him.

'Hey, Mandarin,' said Tony, after Leveque had forced

him to his knees, 'I can tell by the way you use your walk, you're a woman's man, no time for talk.'

The Mandarin considered this while he finished his routine. 'This is true generally,' he said bowing to Tony. 'However, I do find that taking the time to talk is beneficial to a relationship. But I feel you are mocking me, so ...'

The Mandarin raised a fine eyebrow and Leveque dealt Tony a savage blow to the neck.

'Now, now, Freddie,' admonished the Mandarin. 'Not so severe, if you please. Mr Tony Stark will need his wits about him for the morning's activities. I would not wish him to claim that I had an unfair advantage.'

In spite of the vicious blow, Tony's mouth kept running. 'Hey, Mandarin. Is it just Mandarin? Like Prince, or Beyoncé? Or can I call you Mandy?'

The Mandarin squatted before him. 'My family name would have been known to your father, as we were the Asian equivalent of the Starks, you might say. But the communists were covetous of my family's power and violently relieved us of it. Since that day I have been reminding governments of the fragility of their positions.'

Tony coughed blood onto the flagstones. 'Nice justification speech, Mandy. I used to give those to myself in the mirror. Never out in the real world, though – that would be weird.'

If Stark had been hoping to rile his enemy, then he was disappointed. The Mandarin just clapped his hands and smiled broadly.

'Tony Stark, you are somehow a genius and an idiot at the same time. There is no possible advantage with these, as you Americans call them, *wisecracks.* All you do is force me to weaken your body in advance of the combat that is to come.'

'I do not like that word,' said Tony.

The Mandarin shrugged. '*Combat?* I am afraid that it is inevitable.'

'No, the other word: *wisecracks*. This is good material here. Grade A stuff.'

The Mandarin stood, his knees cracking. 'I see how it is, Stark. The idiot has taken over. Such a pity, as the genius might have been of some use to you this morning.'

Leveque grabbed a fistful of Stark's hair and pulled his head back. 'Zis rich man is nuzzink without 'is metal toy,' he said into Tony's ear. 'Zis will not be a contest, chef. It will be a slaughter.'

The Mandarin stretched, reaching overhead with fingers crooked as though he would tear holes in the sky.

'Let us hope so, Freddie. We are on the clock, after all.'

Tony decided he had played the fool long enough for the idea to take hold in the Mandarin's mind, so he asked some pertinent questions.

'So, what? We're fighting to the death now, is that it?'

'That is indeed the case,' said the Mandarin. 'I know it would make more financial sense to ransom you back to your company, but you are a loose end.'

'So I need to be taken care of, right?'

'Precisely.'

'Some kind of respect thing?' said Tony. 'You gotta show the staff how you still got it, right?'

The Mandarin nodded. 'Yes, yes, exactly. A simplistic explanation, but accurate. The power structure of the world I choose to live in is in no way democratic. It is based on fear. These men obey me because they fear me – and because I pay them an exorbitant amount, but fear is the key.'

Tony shook off the effects of Leveque's blow and climbed to his feet. 'And now you feel you have to eat my heart, as it were, and steal my powers.'

'That does not actually work,' said the Mandarin, straight-faced. 'But symbolically, yes. I vanquish my enemies and thereby absorb their reputations at least, and mine grows with it.' He sighed. 'It has become something of a tiresome tradition with this group that I personally hunt down the hostage at the end of each operation. When I extinguish the life in your body, it is nothing personal, you understand? I would much prefer to shoot you in the head now and spare us both the effort.'

'I'll keep that in mind,' said Tony dryly. 'So how do we do this? A throwdown, right here?'

Tony certainly hoped not. He was exhausted and hungry, and the Mandarin seemed in excellent shape – fit and fresh, his skin glowing as though he'd just stepped out of a sauna.

'No, no,' said the Mandarin. 'That would hardly be sporting, and my ancestors have always been hunters. I myself can kill a mockingbird at a hundred paces with a bow and arrow. I remember being so disappointed when I read that American book. Quite the misleading title, I thought. No, to finish you here would be decidedly unsporting, and so I will evacuate my men to ensure that the competition is fair. They will wait for me on the boat while I follow you across the island. Once I have killed you and presented your head as proof of my victory, then we can be on our way. Tradition satisfied, loyalty ensured.'

'Glad to be of service,' quipped Tony. 'And tell me, buddy: what happens if I present *your* head down at the docks? Your guys let me go?'

The Mandarin hid a gentle smile behind his hand. 'Ah, yes, Tony Stark. It is possible, I suppose, that you would triumph. In that event you will simply have bought yourself some few minutes until my men slay you in revenge for the loss of their income stream. So you must run the gauntlet through me and then my small group of soldiers if you are to escape the island.'

'Great,' said Tony. 'A lose-lose situation. My favourite.'

Things were looking grim for Tony Stark, it must be said. Nobody but an idiot would bet against the Mandarin in this dogfight. The terrorist was fit and relaxed. Perhaps Stark had the age advantage by a couple of years, but frankly, judging by appearances, it would not have surprised the Mandarin's men much if he was able to rip Stark's head from his shoulders with his bare hands. It was a David and Goliath situation, except in this modern version, David did not have a sneaky slingshot hidden in his pouch.

Stark could not help considering his imminent decapitation. 'Hey, Mandy, are you planning to bite my head clean off with your pearly whites, or are we getting weapons of some sort?'

'Weapons, of course,' said the Mandarin. 'Sharp blades for the both of us. Prussian sabres. My absolute favourite.'

'That's a little unfair,' commented Tony. 'My favourite sharp implement is the knitting needle. It won't take your head off, but give me a couple of hours and I could knit you a lovely vest.'

The Mandarin wiggled his fingers so the rings caught the sun. 'Count yourself lucky it is simply sabres, Stark. Were I to activate my wondrous rings, I could kill you in many horrible ways.'

'I probably wouldn't notice after the first time.'

The Mandarin actually yawned. 'The idiot part of you is tedious, Stark. But I understand. People deal with their imminent deaths in different fashions, but ultimately they all beg to live. You, too, shall beg.'

'I doubt it, Mandy,' said Tony, and there was resolve in his voice. 'I've been up against tougher customers than you. Dear old dad, for one.'

The Mandarin tugged the rings off his fingers – all except Tony's ring – and handed them to Leveque for safekeeping.

'I was hoping for some meaningful last words,' he said, seeming genuinely disappointed. 'But I see now that you are determined to maintain your cowboy act until the end. How American of you.'

'Sorry to disappoint, Mandy,' said Tony, 'but I have bigger things on my mind than trying to provide wise words for a terrorist's memoirs.'

'Very well, Tony Stark. I will remember you as an idiot to the last, if that is how you wish it.'

Tony grew suddenly tired of the "cowboy act." After all, it was not riling up the Mandarin as he'd hoped. The point of riling someone up was that angry people made rash decisions. But if the desired level of anger was not achieved, then the *riler* was just wasting his breath.

'Okay, Mandarin. Just give me my instructions, and let's get on with this. We both have schedules. You need to blow up a summit, and I need to save one.'

The Mandarin laughed long and hard, clapping his hands in mock tribute. 'Oh, dear me, Tony Stark. Save a summit? You cannot even save poor naïve Saoirse. You have only the slimmest hope of saving yourself.'

'Instructions,' insisted Tony. 'Let's have them. If this is supposed to be a fair fight, you're gonna take off the cuffs at least?'

'Freddie will uncuff you,' confirmed the Mandarin. 'At which point you can do something stupid and be shot on the spot or you can proceed to the western summit two kilometres from here. On the summit you will find an ancient stone seat, the king's seat. And on the seat fresh clothing, food and water will await you – and of course your sabre. I shall join you in one hour for our duel. An idiot-proof plan. And just as well, I think, having gotten to know you.'

Tony nodded slowly, absorbing the instructions, ignoring the jab. 'Two kilometres west. Supplies and a weapon on the stone seat. One hour from right now or one hour from when I reach the stone seat?'

'One hour from now,' said the Mandarin. 'As you say, Tony Stark, we both have schedules. If you are not waiting at the stone seat, then I will unleash my dogs of war, as I do not have the luxury of time to spend hunting you – though a morning hunt would indeed be a pleasure.'

Tony glared at the Mandarin, unconsciously clenching and unclenching his fists as he stared. The look in Tony's eyes was one that his close friend Rhodey had christened Business Time, as in, whenever Tony wore that expression, he was preparing to do whatever had to be done. Playtime was well and truly over.

Freddie Leveque hiked Tony's wrists high behind his back, one last sadistic infliction of pain before unlocking the cuffs. Tony felt the fingers of his own Iron Man gauntlet close painfully around his hand. Thankfully, the servomotors were not operational, or his metacarpals would have been shattered.

'Run, little billionaire,' said Leveque, turning the key.

'Allez vite!'

And for once Tony Stark did not spare time for a withering retort. He simply shambled across the courtyard towards the winding path beyond, and as his kinked and stiff limbs loosened up, his shamble transformed into an all-out sprint.

Two kilometres over rough terrain could take up to fifteen minutes. That left three quarters of an hour to prepare for the man with the big sword.

OH, MANDY

As it turned out, Tony had overestimated his own fleetness of foot, and it took him almost twenty-five minutes to reach the stone seat. The Mandarin had neglected to mention that the last quarter mile of his trek would be a steep climb over loose shale slickened by sea spray even at this altitude.

With each backslide Tony cursed the terrorist, but he drove himself forwards, because this fight was not just about himself. It was about the future of the environment. If the Mandarin succeeded in assassinating the various ministers, it would be decades before such an assembly could be reconvened, and by then it might be too late to save the Arctic glaciers and the ozone layer, to name but two, which would mean the extinction of dozens of species and the displacement of millions of people. As tragic as those scenarios were, right now Tony had to concentrate on the immediate loss of life that would result from his augmented Iron Man suit's dropping in on the summit.

The stone chair put Tony in mind of Arthurian England – as in, this was what Arthur's throne would probably look like if someone had left it exposed to the ferocious elements since Arthur took a shank in the skull from nephew Mordred way back in the sixth century. Perhaps the chair had once been an impressive seat of power, but now it was worn down to a nub of its former self.

'I know how you feel,' Tony said to the seat, displaying a spark of his old gumption even if no one was around to hear it. And he thought that he'd better watch the thinking-out-loud thing, because if Friday wasn't in his ear, then he was just an unkempt guy muttering to himself.

The throne had been carved from the rock itself sometime in the dim and distant past, and it was adorned with panels of Celtic spirals and pictographs that had no doubt once stood out in clear relief but were now dissolving slowly, eroded by salty mist and obscured by fingers of moss. On the seat itself sat a care package in a Red Cross bag. The famous red cross had been crudely augmented with the Mandarin's dragon chest tattoo symbol. Beside the package, glinting sunrise red, stood a long sword.

That thing is humongous, thought Tony. *I might not be able to lift that, never mind swing it with enough force to lop the guy's head off.*

Tony crossed the clearing and tore open the bag. Inside were vacuum-packed foil meals and bottled water.

Stark twisted the cap off the water and raised the bottle to his lips, then paused before drinking as something occurred to him.

'Mandarin,' he said, 'the only thing I know about you is that you don't play fair with friends or enemies. So I wonder how that particular personality defect is manifesting itself today.'

And then he said, 'Tony, baby, you gotta stop talking to yourself. Folks will think you're crazy.'

Some thirty-odd minutes later, the Mandarin strolled easily into the clearing to find Tony Stark lounging on the stone seat, swigging the last from his bottle of water.

'Oh, Mandy,' said Tony. 'You came.'

The Mandarin's smile was a little forced. He was determined to remain gracious, but this American was sorely testing his mood. He cheered himself by visualizing the blade of his sabre cleaving Stark's spine.

'Mr Stark,' said the Mandarin, 'your time is at hand. I do hope the idiot in you took some time off to allow your serious side to make peace with your chosen god.'

Tony stood and did a few stretches. 'You know what, Mandy? I'm feeling better. A lot better. Maybe that water has magical restorative powers.'

'I think not,' said the Mandarin, allowing himself a brief smirk, which did not go unnoticed by his opponent.

'Don't write me off so soon, Mandy,' said Tony, hefting his sword with obvious effort. 'I might surprise you.'

The Mandarin twirled his sabre as though it were light as the oft-referenced feather.

'Your bravado is to be expected. It is basic psychology, in fact. A weak opponent will put on a braggadocious display with the hope of disconcerting his enemy. A vain hope, unfortunately, Mr Stark.'

'Worth a shot,' said Tony. 'But I would add that, in addition to the disconcerting thing, I was also time-wasting.'

The Mandarin assumed a fighting stance. 'A strange tactic indeed, considering the fact that Iron Man will shortly be seen to murder seven environmental ministers and you will be held responsible.'

This remark seemed to press a button. Tony Stark suddenly attacked with considerable speed, forcing the Mandarin to execute an expert parry and sidestep as Stark's sabre came whistling down where his head had recently been.

'Well done, Stark old man,' said the Mandarin. 'You have found some spirit.'

It seemed as though Tony was done talking. He whirled around and launched another offensive, the tendons in his neck standing out as he raised the sword and swung at the Mandarin. It was not an attack of any great finesse, because

Tony had never trained with a sabre, but he did know the basics of fencing thanks to several lessons with Friday, who had studied the teaching methods of David Abramovich Tyshler, widely regarded as the greatest fencing instructor in recent history. So Tony kept his weight low and did not overreach, but other than these two elementary tactics, the Mandarin was his superior in every way.

The Mandarin blocked the blade with his own and the sabers sawed at each other, raising sparks at the contact.

'Ha!' said the terrorist. 'Good.'

The tip of Tony's sword was forced into the earth, and Stark demonstrated his quick thinking by taking one hand from the pommel and rabbit-punching his opponent in the kidney. If this were a training session, he would have followed the opportunistic move with a quip such as 'You like that, Mandy?' but he was in combat mode now. Plus, that particular quip was definitely in the deep end of the lame pool.

The Mandarin grunted and took a half step sideways but was barely inconvenienced.

'Good,' he said again. 'Very good, Mr Stark. Some competition at last.'

Stark used the second he had bought to yank his sword from the earth and strike the Mandarin's kidney again, this time with the sabre's pommel. He was rewarded with a grunt through his opponent's teeth, and no fake congratulations this time. He had hurt his enemy.

The Mandarin recovered quickly, bringing his

elbow in tight to guard the bruised kidney and swinging his other arm around with the sword inverted, its blade hissing as it sliced the air – and not just the air; Tony's shoulder was cut to the bone before he had time to evade the deadly steel.

'Ha!' said the Mandarin, exulting in first blood. 'The end begins.'

Tony gritted his teeth against the sudden almost overwhelming pain. His shoulder felt like a mass of throbbing raw meat, and blood flowed freely down his arm. Tony knew that this gash alone would be enough to kill him should the blood loss cause him to pass out. He pressed on with his attack, jamming the hilt of his sword into the Mandarin's jaw. It was a solid contact and the terrorist was knocked off his feet, but no sooner had his rear end grazed the dirt than he was up again, shaking off the effects of the blow like a dog shaking moisture from its fur.

'That is enough now, I feel,' he said. 'Let us be done with this.'

'Yes,' said Tony. 'Let's.'

Both men attacked, swords raised then brought down with deadly purpose. Five times the blades clashed. Then a dozen. It was medieval brutality with no hope of mercy.

But just as suddenly as it had begun, it seemed as though the combat was over. The exchange seemed to have exhausted and disoriented Tony Stark. He staggered unsteadily, and his eyes darted from left to right as though searching for focus.

The Mandarin noticed and growled low in his throat like a satisfied jungle cat. 'Ah, Tony Stark. You are feeling the strain, I think?'

Stark turned his face to the sound of the terrorist's voice. 'Get back!' he said, and there was a tinge of desperation in his voice. 'I'll kill you.'

'I think not,' said the Mandarin, massaging his jaw. 'You showed some promise, but it is over now.' He circled behind Tony and slapped the billionaire's backside with the flat of his blade, sending Tony tumbling into the brush.

'An ignominious end for the great Tony Stark,' noted the Mandarin. 'Brought low by a single shallow wound.'

'I cannot die,' said Tony, and he seemed on the verge of tears. 'Please.'

'And so you beg,' said the Mandarin. 'As I predicted.'

Tony rolled onto his back, limbs flailing as he tried to scramble away from his enemy, but he could find no purchase in the dew-slick undergrowth. He was a sorry sight, pale and bloodied – a very different man from the one who only moments before had launched himself into battle with such fervour. Indeed, he seemed totally incapacitated by terror and injury, and it was all he could do to lie spread-eagled in the dirt, waiting for the Mandarin's coup de grâce, which, now that the moment had arrived, the Mandarin seemed in no particular hurry to administer. It was almost as if he believed the danger was passed.

'Look at you,' said the Mandarin. 'You can't even lift your sword.'

Tony's only response to this withering observation was to confirm it. His fingers clenched around the weapon's grip, but he did not seem to have the strength to move it.

The Mandarin swished his own sabre through the air, enjoying the blade's hiss.

'I have often wondered how it must feel to see your own death approaching,' he said. 'How you must feel right at this moment. How do you feel, Tony Stark? Can you even tell me that?'

Tony tried to say something, but his mouth flapped pathetically like the gills of a landed fish. Nothing comprehensible emerged.

The Mandarin cleared the brush from around Tony with deft strokes of his sword and then stuck the blade into the earth.

'Allow me to tell you something to make you feel even worse,' he said, kneeling beside Tony to whisper in his ear. 'I do not intend to allow this beheading to go to waste, as it were. In some weeks, once the world knows that the American Tony Stark was responsible for the attack on Dublin, I will release a video of myself, the Mandarin, punishing the assassin. I will be a hero to many. To the rest I shall have become more than a terrorist. A righteous vigilante, perhaps. And there is more I would tell you ...'

Tony took a deep laboured breath. 'Two things,' he said with apparent effort.

The Mandarin nodded, impressed. 'You have some inner strength, Mr Stark. Though I doubt it shall extend to conveying these *two things*.'

Tony coughed, then lifted himself to a sitting position for one more word.

'I know your type, Mandy,' Tony said, and while the Mandarin was busy being irritated by the nickname, he pressed on. 'And I know your type cheats. So I didn't drink the water.'

It had occurred to Tony that a trickster like the Mandarin would gain the upper hand any way he could, including drugging his opponent's precious, life-sustaining water. So Tony had performed a simple pour test on a patch of grass. The grass had turned pale yellow, which should not happen with PH-neutral water, leading him to believe that his bottle was spiked.

'You didn't drink ..." said the Mandarin. 'But that means ...'

'Full sentences, please, Mandy,' said Tony. Then he bashed the Mandarin in the side of the head with his sword – a sword that was not as heavy as Tony had pretended, especially since he had removed the tungsten bar concealed inside the hollow grip. Another of the Mandarin's sneaky tricks.

The Mandarin keeled over, the pain in his head sharper than a lightning strike, but even as he fell, he called out:

'Freddie! *Aidez moi!*'

Tony was not surprised. In fact, he had guessed that

a showboat like the Mandarin would not pass up the opportunity to record the death of such an iconic American. And who else would he bring along but his lieutenant?

Tony stepped hard on the Mandarin's right wrist and twisted his college ring from the terrorist's finger.

'That's mine,' he said, sliding the ring onto his pinky and twisting the crown forty-five degrees before placing his thumb on the crystal. The crown flashed red.

Darn, thought Tony. *I need green.*

The Mandarin was somehow jamming his signal.

'Freddie!' called the Mandarin, even as his eyes rolled back in his head. 'Kill the ...'

Stark punched the Mandarin in the temple before he could complete his order, which Stark figured would probably end with an insult anyway. It was doubtful that the Mandarin's entire sentence would have been something like 'Kill the charming guest to our little terrorist soirée.'

The Mandarin was stunned, probably concussed, but still he managed a few coherent sentences before he passed out completely. 'This changes nothing. Leveque is coming. My trained frog will pounce on you, Stark.'

From the woodland below came a fierce crash and a string of French expletives.

'That's the second thing,' said Tony. 'I moved your snare.'

*

A man like Freddie Leveque would not stay trussed up for long in a simple snare, so Tony stumble-raced across the clearing and down the hillside toward the only spot that had a clear view of the killing ground, where he figured the Mandarin would stash his videographer – the same spot where Tony had rerigged the Mandarin's hunting snare.

Vanity, Mandy, thought Tony as he huffed. *That's your soft spot.*

The Mandarin had made such a point of telling Tony that his ancestors were noble hunters that Tony reasoned there must be a hunter's trick in the mix somewhere. And he found it in the rough border of the clearing: a simple loop feeding back to a log counterweight. If the drugged water and weighted sword had not sufficiently inconvenienced Stark, then the Mandarin would have thrown himself on the ground behind the snare, leading his enemy into the trap. Obviously, Tony could not move the counterweight, but he did manage to rig the snare to a flexible branch that would not provide the snap of a counterweight but should be enough to yank the videographer several feet into the air.

This is all Friday's take on game theory, Tony realized. *Focus on what is not yet in play. Think two steps ahead.*

It would have been so easy for Tony to drink the water and practise with the sword, but instead he had crawled inside the Mandarin's mind.

Thanks, Friday.

But it wasn't Friday. It was Saoirse.

And she was still in danger.

'One thing at a time,' said Tony, breaking his own rule about talking to himself. 'Put on your own oxygen mask before helping children.' Which he thought was a reasonable analogy under the circumstances.

Tony crashed through ragged scrub to find Leveque swearing and inverted, his fingers scrabbling at the earth, perhaps five inches from a huge nickel-plated revolver that glinted enticingly just out of reach. Stark knew enough French to understand what the Mandarin's second-in-command was saying, and the Frenchman's frustration brought a smile to Stark's haggard face.

'*Bonjour*, Freddie,' he said jauntily. 'Ain't it funny how the world turns?'

Leveque used his fingers to set himself swinging back and forth. 'You are dead, Stark. I will crush you!'

This seemed entirely possible, as Leveque's legs were almost as thick as the adjacent tree trunk, and a sprung branch couldn't hold such a muscle-bound lunk aloft forever. So Tony decided not to waste another second on banter and instead grabbed the Iron Man gauntlet, which Leveque was wearing as a trophy, and spun the man in a dizzying circle until the gauntlet came loose. Unfortunately, just as the gauntlet let go, so did the rope, and Leveque yelped once before his momentum sent him tumbling toward a thicket, into which he disappeared. The gauntlet slipped from Tony's hands, spinning into the long grass.

Leveque is unconscious, hopefully, thought Tony. *Stunned, at the very least.*

But there was immediate rustling in the thicket and Tony knew the Frenchman's thick skull had kept him awake.

Merde, he thought, and scrambled after the gauntlet. He had barely lifted it from the earth when Freddie literally exploded from the bushes, borne aloft by his freakishly developed thighs. His hang time seemed to last forever, and the thought popped into Tony's head that Leveque could have a heck of a career in the NBA if he ever turned his back on crime.

Leveque landed with a thump that Tony could've sworn he felt vibrate through the soles of his sneakers.

'I will crush you,' said Leveque again, demonstrating with his spade-like hands.

'You don't have to mime it,' said Tony. 'I know what crushing is.'

'And zat gauntlet will not 'elp you. It is nuzzink but junk. It does not *function*.'

Leveque pronounced *function* in the French manner – *fong-shee-on* – a manner that Tony threw back at him.

'You're right, this particular gauntlet doesn't *fong-shee-on*. Not without its coded failsafe power source.'

This gave Leveque pause. 'Power source. *Quelle* power source?'

And as he said it, Leveque saw the college ring on

Tony's finger – the ring Tony had wrestled from the Mandarin.

'Oh, *non*,' he said.

'Oh, *oui*,' said Tony, and he slipped his hand into the gauntlet. The nanosecond the ring's Vibranium gemstone touched the omnisensor inside the gauntlet, the servomotors hummed to life and Tony Stark was wearing a fully functional Iron Man glove that, though not weaponized, being part of the Party Pack, did feature a repulsor beam that could, when focused, push an object – or in this case, a person.

Leveque's expression underwent a lightning transformation from belligerent to desperate, which involved an almost comical elevation of the eyebrows and flaring of the nostrils. His fight-or-flight instincts took hold, and he decided on *fight*, which, as it turned out, was the wrong decision.

Leveque hurled himself at Tony just as Stark unleashed a blast from his repulsor node. The irresistible force paradox states that when an unstoppable force meets an immovable object, mutual destruction is assured. However, even though the repulsor rays were verging on unstoppable, Freddie Leveque was certainly not immovable. So he was moved very swiftly through the air to the top of the tree he had once dangled from.

'Three points,' said Tony Stark. 'And the crowd goes wild, as well they should. This guy was worth every dime.'

Having satisfied his smart-ass gene, Tony kissed the

knuckle of his gauntlet and hurried down the hill towards the ancient fortress. He almost immediately regretted taking that moment to satisfy his smart-ass gene when he heard a whoosh behind him. Looking over his shoulder, he saw the fizzing ascension of a flare from the treetop where he had deposited the charming Mr Leveque.

No doubt a call to arms for the rest of M Troop.

'Now you are truly dead, Stark!' shouted Freddie Leveque.

People have been telling me that all morning, thought Tony, changing his path and swinging around to the north. He would have to pass the Mandarin again, but Stark felt confident that even if the villain had recovered his senses, he could send him back to the land of nod with a gentle tap from his gauntlet.

He flexed the gauntlet's fingers and was comforted by the gentle whir of servomotors.

Tony's plan had been to pick a spot overlooking the harbour and keep an eye on Spin Zhuk and her unsavory pals until the help he had already summoned arrived. That wouldn't work now. He was being hunted.

I need to keep moving for a few minutes, thought Tony. *And find a hole in the Mandarin's signal shield.*

*

Things were not working out so well for Tony Stark tactically. He had decided to run away from his pursuers to circumvent being shot in a head to which he was very attached. This would seem like a sound plan, but Stark had failed to take into account the simple facts that (1) he was on an island and (2) it might occur to his enemies to split up, which it indeed had. This meant that, although he was actually running away from some of his enemies, he was running towards others. This grew increasingly obvious with every yard he trudged toward the small island's northern cliff face. There was a quad bike coming at him from one side, and he could hear the shouts of his pursuers as they closed the gap.

I can see why this place made such a great prison, Tony thought, changing tack for the umpteenth time. *A tiny island with sheer cliffs along eighty percent of its coastline.*

And while Tony was usually a big fan of wildlife in general and birds in specific, he had to admit the cacophonous screeching of Little Saltee's indigenous gulls was distracting, to say the least.

'Shut up, gulls!' he said, but softly, in case his voice would give away his position – or in case the gulls would poop on him, which was not how he wanted his body to be found, because the world's news agencies would undoubtedly run with that photo. He could imagine the headline:

ELOOLRQDLUH#VRQ|#VWDUN#LV#MXVW#SRRSHG

Or maybe:

IURQ#PDQ#LV#IRU#WKH#ELUGV

That was not how he wanted to be remembered.

The quad bike roared just behind a rocky ridge, and Tony was forced to turn once again. He knew that he was effectively being herded toward the cliffs and that his ring still had not found a signal. Perhaps his technology had malfunctioned.

Which technology hardly ever does, right?

Tony had one repulsor at his disposal, but that was not enough to make him fly and certainly not enough to protect his head from bullets. Against a single opponent he might have stood a chance, but against three at least, all armed to the teeth … even Nick Fury couldn't shoot his way out of this narrow area between a rock and a high place.

He heard shouts to his left … and was that a dog barking?

Where did they get a dog? There hadn't been a dog before. Definitely no fair.

The quad bike roared to his right, with Spin Zhuk's voice somehow rising above it.

'Over here! I see his pointy head.'

Pointy head. Now they were adding insult to injury, with possibly more injury to follow.

Tony had no option but to run straight. And *straight* didn't go on for very long on a small island.

As it turned out, *straight* didn't even last as long as Tony had thought. After fifty or so yards, he found himself teetering on the edge of a sheer cliff, windmilling his arms to avoid plunging into the churning sea below. The movement was a not-so-kind reminder of his wounded shoulder. Even in that painful and stressful moment, he noticed that the waves were much less surfer-friendly than the breakers in Malibu. These weren't so much *breakers* as *crushers.* Nobody was paddling out of a tube in this water saying, 'Dude, that totally rocked. Where's my wax?'

Tony also noticed that as his gauntlet hung there, stretched out over the void, it flashed green for a moment. He had found the edge of the Mandarin's jammer envelope and sent a signal.

Stark righted himself with a blast from his repulsor and turned to face his pursuers.

Come on, cavalry! he thought. *Hurry it up!*

The two pursuers he faced were no more than ten feet away, showing a little more respect than they had earlier in the day, possibly because of the very obviously active Iron Man gauntlet humming on Tony's forearm.

Only two, thought Tony. *I could have taken them.*

But he'd had no way of knowing. The Mandarin could have had a dozen more soldiers.

Spin Zhuk sat hunched behind the handlebars of her quad bike, revving the big machine as though she was going to drive him over the cliff with her front wheels, which she no doubt could if she felt like it. Leveque squatted atop a rock, seeming a mite teed off, which was probably because of the whole treetop thing. There was a guy with something to prove, and Tony knew he would attack the second the order was given.

Then, striding angrily through the undergrowth was the man who would give the order: the mighty Mandarin himself, with an expression pasted across his normally serene features that would paralyze a cow.

'Mandy,' said Tony, 'you seem stressed. You should get a massage.'

The Mandarin hefted his sword, which had yet to drain the blood of a billionaire.

'Yield, Stark. End this foolishness.'

Tony shook his head. 'No yielding for me today. And no respect from the troops for you.'

The Mandarin could not hide his irritation. 'That is not your affair. The team and I will work through our issues. As far as you are concerned, there are two options: you face the inevitable and submit to your decapitation, or you put up a fight and we shoot you, then decapitate your staged corpse. Not ideal, I admit, but better than nothing.'

Neither of these options was great as far as Tony was concerned. After all, both ended with him dead and separated from his head, a head that had been responsible for most of his good ideas.

'There are two more options, Mandy.'

The Mandarin sighed like he was getting fed up with sighing.

'One is you fight, I suppose? Then Freddie will shoot you before you can raise that gauntlet of yours. And the second ...' The Mandarin paused, puzzled. 'What is the second, Mr Stark?'

Tony laughed like he couldn't believe he was about to do what he was about to do.

'The second? Well, this is the second.'

And he stepped backwards over the edge of the cliff as if he were stepping onto a mall escalator.

A LONG WAY DOWN

Dún Laoghaire Harbour, Dublin, eighty miles north of Little Saltee

The "cavalry" that Stark was relying on had been flipping an omelet for a pop star – a rubber omelet for a robotic pop star. But a nanosecond after Tony's coded secure distress signal got through to the Prototony's operating system, the android froze like a deer sensing danger and seemed to sniff the air.

The Prototony dropped the spatula and tore off his apron. 'I do apologize, Shoshona,' he said to the artificial girl in the golden bikini, 'but I am needed elsewhere. Urgently needed, in fact. Sometimes only Tony will do.'

Even robot Stark was a smart-ass.

Following an expedited flight check, the Prototony

blasted off from the deck into the morning sky, literally shedding his skin – and his apron – as he flew. Strips of plasti-skin peeled away from the android's skull as he neared the sound barrier, revealing the helmet of an Iron Man suit beneath. That explained why Friday – or Saoirse, to be accurate – had believed the Prototony a little bulky: there was a functional flight suit hidden beneath the skin, another fact the paranoid billionaire had kept to himself.

This particular one was an emergency Medi-suit tailored specifically to Tony Stark's anticipated needs. It was, if you like, a sophisticated ambulance – albeit an ambulance with two weeks' worth of life support in its battery.

In spite of the dozens of cameras trained on the *Tanngrisnir* at that moment, only one photographer was sharp enough to snap a picture of the Prototony's dramatic liftoff, and when he scrolled back to check his prize, he found himself looking at what appeared to be a flying chef.

Digital glitch, he thought in disgust, and deleted the frame.

The Prototony locked on to Tony's signal and noted his elevated pulse and blood pressure. He saw that Tony was wounded, dehydrated and fatigued, and placed him in the category *distressed*, which was a delicate way of putting it. The suit quickly accelerated towards the sound barrier and just as quickly decelerated, as enveloping the principle at that speed would break every bone in his body.

The suit's approach speed was not the only difficulty. Though Mr Stark's initial velocity had been a convenient zero feet per second, it was now fluctuating wildly, as was his trajectory, making docking calculations very complicated and decidedly unreliable. In short, the suit was having to make its best guess.

A couple of things were, however, all too certain.

One: it would have to be a sub-aquatic pickup.

And two: bones would shatter.

For the optimum pickup angle, Prototony dipped under the water's surface while he was still two kilometres from the calculated interception.

Tony did everything he could to slow his descent with one repulsor, but he really shouldn't have bothered. Any cliff diver could have told him that he would've been better off making like a pencil and cutting into the water, not pinwheeling through the air like a crazed firework. This was not the first time Stark had crash-landed in water, but last time he had been wearing a full battle suit and had barely felt the impact.

In fact, Rhodey had been with him on the previous occasion, which had been a suit demo off the Malibu Pier for a children's charity. Iron Man and War Machine had blasted each other with flash bangs for a few minutes and were about to launch into a choreographed dogfight when Tony's systems had suddenly frozen, sending the billionaire plummeting into the Pacific. Rhodey had laughed his head off while he fished Tony out of the surf and delivered him back to the workshop.

'Man, you're lucky the suit held up,' he'd said between chortles. ''Cause from that altitude, water feels like concrete.'

Tony had laughed then, too.

He wasn't laughing now.

The world flashed by in a kaleidoscope of blues and greens, and he barely had enough time to get his head up before he crashed into the surf feet first – feet that were protected only by pumped-up running shoes. The sneakers' air-filled soles burst with a sound like a pistol shot, and then both ankles snapped; the left tibia and right fibula went milliseconds after, and Tony Stark lost the ability for rational thought as his entire world became a vista of pain. A single word chased itself around his head over and over.

Sorry. Sorry. Sorry.

Tony would later wonder what he felt sorry for at the supposed moment of his death, but he would never be able to narrow it down to just one thing. Eventually, he would open up enough to talk about it with Rhodey, who would comment, 'It doesn't matter what you're sorry about, bro. What matters is that you change your life enough so the next time you're about to check out you feel better about yourself.'

To which Tony would respond, 'Thanks a bunch,

Oprah.'

To which Rhodey would take offence, and the two buddies would start wrestling in the den and knock a priceless Oliver Jeffers original dipped painting off the wall.

But back to the crushing impact into the unforgiving Atlantic Ocean. Stark would have gone into shock and drowned had not the Iron Man Medi-suit matched his sink rate, scooped him up at ten fathoms – two fathoms above the underwater crags on which his body would surely have been impaled – and literally folded its reversible self inside out, cocooning the billionaire's body in a protective layer of armour. In a matter of seconds, the interior of the suit was flooded with oxygen-rich air, and a thousand sensors scanned the patient's body for traumas, of which they found plenty. Both legs of the suit inflated cast cushions that manipulated Tony's bones into their proper place and secured them there. Microneedles pumped anaesthetic into the trauma sites, and a larger needle jabbed a large dose of adrenaline into Stark's chest, dragging him out of the valley of shock into which he had been sinking.

'Sorry!' he blurted one last time, then came back to the present and realized that the Medi-suit was blasting towards the surface now that he had been stabilized.

'No,' he said.

To which the Prototony said, '*No?* No to what, Tony?

I'm doing a lot of stuff here.'

'No to surfacing,' said Tony, mightily relieved that the pain was subsiding. 'Keep the suit submerged for the moment.'

'Not a good idea, Tony baby,' said Prototony. 'We've got maybe five minutes of breathables in this suit. After that, you're sucking fumes.'

'Do what I say,' snapped Tony, possibly made a touch irritable by the cliff fall and the broken bones. 'Who is this, anyway? Which AI?'

'It's me. I mean, you. Or superficial public you, at any rate. The one beloved by paparazzi the world over. My behaviour is learned from Internet footage of you, which makes me quite the shallow guy, which is funny at the moment, considering where we are. Get it?'

Tony groaned with residual pain and mental anguish. Maybe it was true what Rhodey said about him.

I am *a pain in the butt,* he realized. *And does my voice* really *sound like that? I thought it was deeper.*

'Do we have access to another AI?'

'Sorry, Tony baby, this is it. You're stuck with me. This suit is a pretty basic model. Designed to get you home and that's it. A flying stretcher.'

A flying stretcher, thought Tony. *Far from ideal, but it will have to do.*

'Okay. I'm overriding your mission parameters,' he said. 'Keep us submerged for as long as possible, then full speed for Dublin docklands. I need to catch someone.'

'You got it, Tony,' said Prototony. 'Who are we chasing?'

'Me. We're chasing me.'

'Hey,' said Prototony, 'that makes three of us.'

On the Little Saltee cliff top, Spin Zhuk nudged her quad bike to the edge and peered over.

'I cannot believe this man did such a thing,' she said. 'The idiot forgot he could no longer fly.'

' 'E is terrified, *non*?' said Freddie Leveque. 'Zat is it. 'E prefers ze quick fall.'

The Mandarin said nothing for a while, simply stroking his moustache thoughtfully.

'I think that Mr Stark preferred to choose his own fate,' he said finally, 'rather than accept the one I had chosen for him. Perhaps he was not the idiot I believed him to be.'

'Ze man jumped from a cliff,' said Leveque. 'Zerefore, he is ze idiot.'

The Mandarin squinted at him. 'Are you serious, Freddie? *Zerefore?* Remember that Stark bested us both, if temporarily. And without his marvellous suit.'

Leveque shrugged. 'Perhaps. But 'e is dead now, so not so clever, eh?'

'It does not matter,' said the Mandarin. 'Stark is dead. We still have a green light. Tell the boat to watch the impact spot for five minutes, then return to the dock. After that, complete radio silence. Not so much as a text to your loved ones until after the mission is complete. One message is enough to triangulate us all. We will give our Pyro one hour to complete his mission and return here. If he does not, then we leave without him.'

'And the girl?' asked Spin Zhuk. 'What should we be doing with her?'

The Mandarin held out a hand to Leveque, who returned his rings to him.

'Do you perhaps think that something has changed, Miss Zhuk?'

Spin Zhuk was no wilting wallflower and had in her time taken down an entire team of Russian Spetsnaz troopers, armed with only a spork and two hairpins, but she was not brave enough to hold the Mandarin's glare.

'No, chef. I am not thinking this thing.'

The Mandarin had a point to make. 'Perhaps you believe that because Stark chose the coward's way out rather than face me, somehow my authority is compromised?'

Zhuk paled and shook her head. 'No, chef. I would never believe this. I would *never* believe it. I am only alive on this day because of you. My life is yours.'

'Well then, Miss Zhuk, why do you ask me this question? You know full well what must happen to the girl, do you not?'

Leveque was eager for blood. 'Allow me, chef. I am in ze terrible mood.'

'No, Freddie,' said the Mandarin. 'Miss Zhuk asked

the question, and now she must answer it with steel.'

Zhuk swallowed but did not object. If she objected, she would be taking the same route as Stark had over the cliff's edge.

'I will do it, chef,' she said. 'Consider it done.'

'Good, excellent,' said the Mandarin, his mood restored. 'Make it quick. Or slow, as you like. We have an hour.'

Quick, Zhuk decided. It would definitely be quick.

She opened the quad bike's throttle and roared along the coastline towards the medieval prison before she could change her mind.

Teenagers suffer from many common ailments: acne, asthma and negative body image, to name a few. But the adolescent trait that tends to drive the rest of the population's blood pressure skyrocketing is their tendency to *know it all*. There is even a medical term for it: *metacognitive naïvety*. This is where teenagers do not consider their thoughts to be possible interpretations of events but direct lines into the *truth soul* of the planet. Most teens are gently moved away from *know-it-allness* by the simple process of growing up and all the emotional upheaval contained therein, but Saoirse Tory was about to be traumatically cured of metacognitive naïvety by being killed to death.

The ironic thing was that recent events had already set her on the road to recovery, so a cure was not technically necessary.

Though I doubt the Mandarin will take that into account, Saoirse thought now, waiting for the terrorist's lackeys to come back and carry out her sentence.

Saoirse knew all about metacognitive naïvety but did not believe that she herself suffered from it, as she actually *did* know it all. Or she *had* known it all before the Mandarin turned her ingenious plan inside out. This depressed the Irish girl for a while, until she realized that *actually* the Mandarin had not turned her plan inside out; he had just piggybacked on it for his own ends.

So in fact, my plan was a work of total genius.

This cheered her up until she remembered that Tony Stark was more than likely dead because of her, and soon several environmental ministers would be joining him in the afterlife.

Not that I'll live to see any of that, she recognized gloomily.

She fantasized about taking the floor in a European court and explaining how none of this was her fault, as in fact she had just been trying to save her sister, Liz, and some African girls.

Maybe I do *suffer from metacognitive naïvety after all,* she realized.

The plucky part of Saoirse's personality reared its irrepressible head.

Get up, girl. No one is dead yet. Maybe Stark escaped. And maybe he'll save the day. Do you want to go to your grave with all those souls on your conscience? Especially if they might not even be dead yet and you could save them?

No, she decided emphatically. She did not.

So, how to get out of there? There must be a way for a smart girl like herself to outwit a couple of terrorists.

As it turned out, there was only one terrorist to outwit: Spin Zhuk, who had been sent to kill the young patsy Saoirse Tory. Spin's heart was not in the job. Not that she hadn't killed before, but she was more of a wheel spinner than a trigger puller.

They are not calling me Pull Zhuk, after all.

She was annoyed with the Mandarin for this misuse of resources but quickly cut off that train of thought, for many believed that the Mandarin could read minds, and he would not brook insubordination, even the mental kind.

But it was difficult not to be unhappy with the assignment.

After all, who wanted to kill a kid?

Nobody, that was who. Except maybe Freddie Leveque, who was never happier than when he was strangling someone with his bare hands.

'Zere is nozink like zat feeling of life leaving ze body,' he had told her one day recently, repeating it several times until she understood.

Spin shuddered. *Life leaving ze body*. She had no intention of experiencing that feeling. A quick shot in the head from behind was how she intended to dispatch the kid. The Irish girl would never even see it coming. Spin parked her quad in the courtyard and walked briskly and with intent across the salt-coated flagstones. The prison must have been some operation back in the day, but now it was falling apart. The constant pound of surf was literally shaking the place to its foundations. The humans had been driven out decades before – all except Saoirse Tory and her crazy grandfather – and in another century there would probably be nothing left above sea level for the gulls to nest on.

This place is driving me *crazy,* thought Spin, *with the screeching and the pooping and the vibrations. I cannot wait to be gone.*

The best idea, she decided, would be to take the girl down to the harbour on the pretense of loading her on the boat. Then a quick pop, and into the water she'd go.

Simple and tidy. Not even a body to be buried.

I am hoping she is falling facedown, Spin thought, *so I am not having to look at the eyes.*

And then she thought, *Why am I thinking in English? I need a holiday in Kiev.*

Spin paused at the ramp that led down to the cell area and patted the Sig Sauer P220 holstered under her shoulder.

Don't let me down, baby, she broadcast at the pistol. But she knew it would not. The Sig had seen her safely through countless altercations and would perform this task without hesitation.

I am the one who will hesitate, she realized.

All thoughts of hesitation vanished suddenly when Spin trotted down the ramp to see Saoirse Tory's cell without Saoirse in it. Spin's first thought was one of those irrational mind farts the brain throws up in times of panic.

The Irish girl has disappeared. She is a fairy leprechaun.

'Leprechaun!' she blurted.

Her next thought was slightly more sensible.

Under the bunk. The girl hides underneath the bed.

Spin was angry with herself for shouting out *leprechaun* and instantly transferred her annoyance to Saoirse.

'Stupid child!' she said. 'You are making my job easier.'

Zhuk went into the cell angry, but even when angry she was no amateur; she drew her pistol, ready for surprises.

'Okay, kid. Be coming out from under there.'

No kid emerged, and there was nowhere else she could be. The cell was three stone walls and a fourth wall of bars, with one army cot in the middle of the floor. Spin considered shooting through the bed itself, which would surely neutralize anyone who was hiding underneath, but shooting a bed would be tantamount to admitting that a mere child could unnerve her. Instead, she grabbed the edge of the bed and wrenched it upward, which was exactly what the girl had wanted her to do.

It had occurred to Saoirse Tory about thirty minutes before Spin Zhuk came down the steps that she herself had been a little worried about the springs in the cell's bedframe when Tony Stark had been a prisoner.

You mean back when the man was alive? whispered her conscience, but Saoirse ignored it, electing to focus on the current opportunity: springs.

Springs could absorb and store energy and had a certain amount of elasticity, so they were potential tools in the hands of a man like Stark. She had allayed her own fears by keeping eyes on Stark for the duration of his imprisonment. But now there were no eyes on her and she had the same potential tools in her hands. And was she not the girl who had outsmarted the smarty-pants?

With industrious determination Saoirse had unclipped the springs and formed a rope, which she had secured at both ends to the bed frame after looping it around one of the cell bars. Then, using all her strength, Saoirse had hiked the bed backwards inch by inch until the springs hummed in protest like banjo strings. When she could go no farther, Saoirse had anchored two legs of the bed in the flagstone grooving and kicked dust over the visible springs. The dust was not magic, so it didn't make the spring rope invisible, but if you weren't looking for it you might not see it.

She'd stood back and surveyed her little trap.

'This is ridiculous, Saoirse,' she had said aloud, unaware that just recently another genius type in the vicinity had been talking to himself and making traps. 'When Tony Stark was in Afghanistan, he built the Iron Man prototype out of some aluminium foil and a triple

A battery, and what are you building? A spring bed. You should be ashamed to call yourself an inventor. There's a one-in-a-million chance that this will work. And even if it does, there might be more than one terrorist still on the island, and even if by some miracle there is only one, the springs might do nothing more than give them a pain in the neck. And I don't mean literally, more's the pity.'

Then she'd heard Spin Zhuk's footsteps tapping their way downstairs and so had dropped to the stone floor and wiggled her torso oh so carefully under the bed, all too aware that one stray knock would set off the springs.

'Careful now, Saoirse girl,' she had whispered, and then stopped talking to herself altogether. After all, she was trying to give the impression that she wasn't there.

Spin Zhuk flipped the bed and saw Saoirse Tory lying underneath, just as she had suspected.

'Aha!' Spin had planned to say. 'You cannot be fooling me with the childish trickery.'

That was the plan all right, but what she actually said was, *'Ah … oooooooorgh,'* with a little spit at the end of it, for the bedspring plan worked better than Saoirse could have hoped despite its inherent dopeyness. When the legs popped out of the slab grooving, the tension in the springs caused the metal to contract desperately, making the frame bunny-hop at a pretty miserable rate of acceleration that would have caused Spin Zhuk zero discomfort had it not been for one thing: the frame hit her square in the throat, almost crushing her trachea. And there is not a creature on the planet that can shake off a metal bar to the trachea, hence the *'Ah ... oooooorgh.'*

'Sorry,' said Saoirse. Then she was up and out the door, taking full advantage of whatever head start the spring trap had earned her.

I should have locked the cell door, she thought halfway up the ramp, with a square of daylight looming temptingly above her. But then a bullet knocked a chunk of rock from the arch over her head and all Saoirse's thoughts were replaced with a single imperative: *Run!*

Obviously, Spin Zhuk's injury had not inconvenienced her as much as Saoirse had hoped.

Saoirse raced up the ramp into the morning sunshine and was relieved to find that there were no more terrorists to dodge for the moment.

If the courtyard had been stuffed with the Mandarin's gang, then that would have been the end of my little escape attempt.

Saoirse had been afraid of a terrorist welcome, but if she was honest with herself, her darkest fear was that she would find Tony Stark's body strung from the battlements, dead eyes staring at her accusingly.

'You did this, you eejit,' the raven on his shoulder would probably say. 'You did this.'

Saoirse banished these thoughts and concentrated on running. Spin Zhuk was mere steps behind, and the bullets in her pistol could travel at over a thousand metres per second, as opposed to her own running speed, which was probably a pathetic ten kilometres per hour or so.

Yes, but bullets can only travel in straight lines, thought Saoirse, ducking through the collapsed arch and swinging a right, hugging the prison's outer wall. Now Spin would have to get really close before she could get a clear shot.

And this is my island, she thought. *I know every headland and rock pool.*

More important for the plan she was developing on the hoof, Saoirse Tory knew the blowhole sequence.

And what's a blowhole?

Hopefully, Spin Zhuk would not know.

RUNNING THE BLOWHOLES

While Saoirse was running for her life around the Little Saltee prison's perimeter wall, Tony Stark was flying in his airborne life jacket towards Dublin's docklands, where no doubt Cole Vanger was closing in on the eco summit, laden with deadly cargo.

'We could just ping the suit,' suggested Prototony. 'Then I can plot a course right to her.'

'My god, you are so dense,' snapped the real Tony. 'That suit is loaded with sensors. If we ping the suit, the suit will know. If the suit knows, then Vanger knows I am on his tail and he will go operational.'

'He's pretty operational already,' said Prototony, a bit sulkily.

'You can sulk now?' said Tony. 'What kind of tone is

that? I don't sound like that.'

'It's one of my learned behaviours. For when Shoshona doesn't like her omelet or something like that.'

Tony rolled his eyes and flew onwards, his altitude so low he almost skimmed the wave tops. Flying in the swell was slower and trickier, but it meant he was virtually indistinguishable from a dolphin or small craft even if Vanger was keeping watch, which he probably was not. And there was no AI on board to run a scan for Mr Pyro.

'Stay off-line,' Tony ordered his Medi-suit. 'Plot a course from onboard maps. We'll have to rely on direct line of sight.'

'Human vision?' said Prototony, horrified. 'What is this, the Stone Age? I have perfectly good prism lenses, installed for picking out survivors in rough seas. Why don't we break out those bad boys?'

'Two things,' said Tony. 'First, never use the words *bad boys* again. You make me sound like a total jerk. And second, good idea. Go ahead and break out those bad boys.'

'I've got a question for you, boss,' said Prototony. 'You're rocking this lightweight gear, and Vanger is packing serious firepower. How do you plan to stop him, even if we do get there in time?'

'I won't be kicking him with my broken legs, that's for sure,' said Tony.

'You're avoiding the question, which does make you seem like a jerk. Don't you have any ideas?'

'I have a couple,' said Tony. 'But they both end up with me being dead, which is not exactly an ideal scenario.'

'Keep thinking then, T-Star.'

'*T-Star?* What in god's name is a T-Star?'

'It's your showbiz name. You take your first initial and add it to the first syllable of your second name. My showbiz name would be P-Tone, which is pretty cool. You can use that if you want.'

'Gee, thanks, P-Tone. Are we, like, BFFs now?'

'T-Star and P-Tone. It doesn't get any tighter.'

'I guess you don't do sarcasm, Prototony?'

'Nope. I'm sunny and current. I'm programmed to be permanently in Tony the Playboy mode. Just as the media might expect.'

'Great. And whose genius idea was this? Mine, I suppose. Great move, wonder boy.'

The Prototony upped the air-conditioning, wafting cool air across Tony's damp brow. 'Don't be so hard on yourself. You're grumpy because your legs are shattered and you weren't expecting to fly a mission in this suit. But I gotta tell you something, T-Star.'

'Please don't.'

'I am beyond excited. P-Tone and the big guy on an adventure together. This is going to be epic. Us fighting ourselves. A bit like when Brienne of Tarth fought the Hound.'

'What are you babbling about?'

'*Game of Thrones*. Hello? Brienne is like lady Dolph

Lundgren, and the Hound is angry *Everybody Loves Raymond*'s brother.'

Tony felt like crying. His legs were beginning to ache and this demented AI that he himself had programmed was force-feeding him entertainment trivia.

'Okay. Whatever. A grand adventure.'

'All for one, T-Star,' the Prototony enthused.

'If we go down, we go down together, right?'

'Not exactly. Your body will be crushed and burned beyond recognition. I've been backed up onto the *Tanngrisnir*'s system.'

'So much for "all for one".' With a swipe of his glove Tony pulled up coordinates on his visor. 'This is roughly where we need to be. It was supposed to be my holding spot while security scanned me for weaponry. Vanger will have to hold in that position or they'll blast him out of the sky. What's our ETA?'

'Entertainment awards? I don't think we have any.'

'ETA!' shouted Tony. 'Estimated time of arrival. You better wake up, P-Tone, or I'm gonna melt you down if we survive this.'

'Wow. Someone needs a latté. Okay, Mr Short Fuse. ETA four minutes.'

Four minutes, thought Tony. *That's pretty quick. That's most definitely in the immediate future.*

'Okay, give me whatever anaesthetic and painkiller we have in the tank, and pump up my casts to maximum pressure.'

Prototony obeyed the command. 'It sounds like

someone has a plan.'

'I wish,' said Tony miserably. 'I think my subconscious is onto something, but it won't let me in on it until the last minute. Probably because it's so monumentally stupid.'

'I thought that *I* was your subconscious,' said Prototony, sulking again.

Tony felt the local anaesthetic flowing like ice water through his legs and he knew that he would have to operate the suit entirely with hand gestures.

'Well,' he said, 'if that's the case, then send out the funeral invites, because we're dead.'

'You can be cruel, Tony Stark. Did anyone ever tell you that?'

Tony chuckled. 'Yeah. My dad's secretary, about a million years ago.'

Little Saltee

Saoirse Tory had spent every free moment on Little Saltee with her grandfather, and it was he who had taught her how to splice ropes, how to bait a lobster pot and how to run the blowholes.

'Running the blowholes. That was our sport, back in the old days,' Francis Tory had told her. 'The golden days, if you ask me, before television got all those stations and children stopped eating lard. No one ever died doing it, and broken bones heal, don't they?'

Most kids would have closed their ears as soon as television started getting disrespected, but Saoirse had loved her granddad so much she would have listened intently to him reading the ingredients for tinned soup.

'There's a line of blowholes along the rocks between the harbour and White Rock. The idea was for a group of us youngsters to pelt along at high tide and avoid the geysers. It's all about timing.'

'Did you ever win, Granddad?' Saoirse had often asked him, to which he would invariably pretend to be offended.

'Did I ever win? Did this fella here ever win? I'm only the blooming record holder. Thirty seconds flat and still with dry britches. Olympics, my backside. I'd love to see that Quicksilver fella run the blowholes. That would sort him out.'

So now Saoirse Tory would run the blowholes, but not just to beat her granddad's record. This time her life was at stake and possibly other lives as well.

Saoirse balled her fists, bore down on her resolve and swung away from the shelter of the prison's outer wall and onto the wide flat shelf of granite. It rumbled with the passage of the Celtic Sea below and was pocked with a thousand treacherous rock pools.

Thirty seconds, she thought. *The longest half minute of my life. Or maybe the last one.*

Spin Zhuk had completely forgotten her earlier squeamishness.

This child is causing such trouble with her ridiculous springs.

Ridiculous but effective. The Mandarin's disciples had spent so much time ensuring that Tony Stark did not escape that they had neglected to pay much attention to the child, and now she was gone.

No. Not gone. Running.

It seemed impossible that the Irish girl could escape. She had made a basic error in leaving cover. All Spin needed now was a clear shot. The only thing that prevented her taking the shot was the fine saltwater mist that fizzed over the rocks, recharged by the crashing waves.

A little closer, thought Spin. *This is all I need to be. Ten seconds and it is done.*

She followed Saoirse, running sure-footedly and without hesitation. As a child she had played on Kiev's Zamkova Hora hill, so this flat stretch of rock presented little challenge.

Strange, though, how the surface shook with the force of the ocean and how a low grumbling emanated from the rock chimneys like the mutterings of a dreaming ogre.

Spin raised her weapon but did not fire. Not yet. On such a small island, the Mandarin would hear the shot, and if a second shot was needed, he would wonder why. Then she would be forced to admit she was in pursuit, and the entire embarrassing story would come out. And perhaps the Mandarin would be displeased. So one shot only, and she was not yet certain of her target, as now the infuriating girl was jinking from side to side in an unpredictable fashion – almost as if she did not wish to be killed.

Or perhaps she is expecting something.

At this moment, underneath the rock shelf, a low wave thundered in from the ocean and rolled through the cavity below – that one-in-ten perfect wave to fuel the blowholes. Then, as countless waves before it had, it punched the cave wall and its tremendous force was dispersed back along the shelf, sending columns of water shooting up through a dozen fissures to the surface.

The sound is changing, thought Spin Zhuk. *The ogre has awoken.*

Up ahead, Saoirse banked left a millisecond before a jet of hissing white water erupted where her feet had been. A moment later, another spout burst from a fissure, but Saoirse dodged that one, too, and Spin Zhuk could have sworn the girl was laughing.

Crazy, thought Spin. *The child is crazy.*

Then, with barely a hiss of warning, a waterspout erupted between Spin Zhuk's feet and blasted along the length of her frame, cracking her jaw shut and knocking the gun from her hand. Spin staggered backward, which turned out to be a bad move, because she more or less sat on another waterspout, which lifted her bodily into the air. Fully ten feet up she went, flailing inside the translucent serpent until she managed to tumble herself out of its wet coils and flop breathless onto the slickened rocks.

Two ribs cracked, she thought when the blowholes finally

quieted and her breath returned. *Two ribs at least.*

But there was nothing to be done for cracked ribs except to bind them, which she would do later and in secret.

Spin rolled onto her side and looked to where the Irish girl had been.

She winced in frustration and pain.

Saoirse had disappeared. Of course. This was her island, and the resourceful girl would lose herself in it and never be found by a stranger.

What now?

How would Spin keep herself alive? First she had questioned the Mandarin, and now she had failed him. The Mandarin tested those who questioned him, but he did not tolerate failure. Legend had it that her boss had once strangled a lackey for serving him cardamom tea instead of hibiscus flower.

Spin saw that her Sig Sauer had skittered no more than ten feet, so as quickly as her injuries and shakiness allowed, she hobbled across the rocks, snagged her weapon and hurried away from the aquatic minefield before the blowholes could assault her once more.

The girl was gone. And if she had sense, she would stay gone – hidden until her enemies had left.

As far as anyone needed to know, the Irish child was dead. For if Saoirse Tory had died on these rocks, then Spin Zhuk would live.

Spin Zhuk cocked her weapon and fired a single shot

into the morning sky.

Cole Vanger hovered over Dublin's docklands convention centre, with its distinctive glass-fronted atrium that bisected the building like a futuristic beer keg, criss-crossed with stairways and railings. The atrium had been specially modified to allow Iron Man access through the roof panels so he could descend slowly into the structure itself, down all eight floors, and land on a specially commissioned Ceadogán green earth rug, around which the environment ministers would be congregated, politely applauding. It would make for most excellent TV.

'Idiots,' said Vanger under his breath, though he should not have said even that much. There were so many lasers scanning his suit now that barely a square inch was left unstrobed. Target lock had been acquired by two gunships in the harbour, and the Royal Air Force had been given special permission to hold a couple of Tornado jets two klicks out with missiles at the ready. Cole Vanger knew this was all pretty much standard security procedure, but he couldn't help taking it a little personally, all the same.

Each time a probe pinged the armour, the Iron Man sensors registered it, identified its source, and fed back the information that the scanning agency would expect to record. With all the computer alerts, he felt like he was hovering inside a xylophone.

'Idiots,' said Vanger again; he couldn't help it. How did these fools believe that their inferior technology could in any way outfox Stark's mechanical marvel?

He felt like a god hovering above these unimportant ants. He longed to unleash the flamethrowers concealed in his gauntlets and watch the ants curl and squirm.

I am the god of fire, he thought, and the notion pleased him. *How can Stark want to serve these people when he could rule them?*

The Mandarin had rigged the suit so it would seem perfectly safe to anyone scanning it. No weapons would show up, naturally. Who would bring concealed weapons to an eco summit? The suit displayed Tony Stark's bio readings, and a vocoder would transform Vanger's voice so it was indistinguishable from Stark's. Vanger had even studied Stark's glib speech patterns so the content of any communications would not raise flags.

Vanger could see them now through his helmet's most excellent lenses: the snipers, the tight bunches of various police units, the world's press eagerly awaiting the arrival of the great Tony Stark.

Get ready, fools, thought Vanger. *The world is about to be changed forever, and you are about to bear witness. Those of you who survive.*

The call he had been waiting for finally came through from Irish security.

'Dublin calling, Mr Stark. Inspector Conroy's the name. Is that you in there, Tony?'

Vanger accepted the call with a blink.

'It sure is, buddy. Who were you expecting,

Santa Claus?'

The security officer laughed. 'Well, sure. You're a bit of a rogue and all that. Maybe you lent the rig out to one of your showbiz friends. It could be yer man Bruce Springsteen in there for all I know.'

Vanger vowed that he would make sure to burn this man. 'Check your scans, pal. One hundred percent Tony Stark.'

'Hey, listen, while I have you on the line: you couldn't let me have Taylor Swift's number, could you? I'm a bit of a fan. Can't get enough of the shaking it off. And I don't even know what I'm shaking off, if you know what I mean.'

'I'll see what I can do, friend. Now, I think we have some environmental ministers waiting?'

'Right you are, Tony boy. Let's blow the roof off this old greenhouse. Come in at your own pace. You're cleared for landing, as the fella said.'

Vanger scowled behind the faceplate. This did not seem like regulation security jargon from Inspector Conroy, but then again he was about to go a little off book himself and unleash a tsunami of napalm and fire inside the atrium. The glass would melt like plates of ice on a barbeque grill.

Vanger knew the names they called him behind his back: *Firestarter. Matches boy. Fire bug*. All to belittle his pyromania, to make it seem weak and unimportant.

After today I will be taken seriously. Because I will have made my hellish mark.

Vanger smiled fiercely and throttled back on the repulsors, gently lowering the Iron Man suit towards the pane in the atrium's roof that was sliding open to grant him access.

They will all burn for the Mandarin's glory, he thought. *And Iron Man will rise from the pyre of their charred bones, forever branded as a terrorist. Branded by Pyro.*

Tony was just in time to realize he was too late.

He cursed and then said to himself, 'Vanger is inside the convention centre.'

The situation was even worse than Stark had anticipated. Normally when Iron Man showed up at a shindig, the public also showed up in droves, which usually stoked Tony's ego to what Rhodey called Diva Level Four. That day he had been hoping for a smaller turnout, given the potential for carnage, but it seemed that Iron Man was just as popular on this side of the Atlantic as he was in sunny California. If anything, he seemed *more* popular. The entire dockland was swamped with cheering crowds, and the famous Samuel Beckett Bridge, with its harp-shaped cabling, seemed too fragile to support the thousands of civilians teeming across it.

My god, thought Tony. *The human collateral damage would be unthinkable. Vanger could take down half the city.*

Prototony butted in on his thoughts. 'I think he's unsheathing.'

It was true. Through the glass panes, Tony could see

the armour peeling back on Vanger's gauntlets, revealing the nozzles of his beloved fire breathers underneath. Twin blue pilot lights appeared at the tips.

'Put me through to him,' commanded Tony.

'I don't see what for,' said Prototony. 'This guy isn't for talking down.'

'I'm not trying to talk him down,' said Tony. 'I'm trying to distract him.'

'Putting you through now, T-Star.'

'And how about a little combat music?'

'Any particular request?'

Tony didn't have to think about it for long. It was time to bring out his fight song of choice.

'Oh, I think we need something Canadian.'

Cole Vanger was feeling all-powerful, as though the fuel in his pipes was his own life's blood. In a metaphorical way it was, because Vanger had spent years tweaking his very own flamethrower cocktail, which included oil, napalm and a smidge of jet fuel. It came out of the nozzle clean and would burn a hole through sheet steel. And inside this structure, which was basically an oven, his unholy flames would scour these people down to the very bone. But not Vanger; he would be safe in the suit, and he thought that those moments, inside his beloved fire, would be the happiest of his life.

Vanger activated his pilot lights and was literally one inch from unleashing fiery hell when an anthemic guitar riff burst from his earpieces.

Cole Vanger knew the classic rock piece – "Tom Sawyer" by Rush.

'What is this?' he shouted.

The volume in his ears was deafening. Who could hijack this helmet?

Cole Vanger's sudden suspicion was confirmed by the voice in his ears.

'I bet you're putting it together right about now, Vanger,' said Tony Stark, who had somehow escaped his fate.

'Stark!' roared Vanger, furious that his moment was being delayed. 'Where are you?'

'Why don't you look up and find out, sparky?'

Vanger obligingly did as he was told, which was when the Iron Man Medi-suit crashed through the atrium at ground level and blindsided Vanger from below.

Classic Stark misdirection.

*

Tony was all, 'I bet you're putting it together …' and 'Why don't you look up and find out, sparky?' The usual patter, in other words. But inside the ambulance suit he was sweating mightily and feeling very uncertain about his imminent future and that of the thousands of spectators.

All Vanger needs to do is get off one burst from his flamethrowers and there'll be a wide swath of casualties.

And even though he wouldn't be pulling the trigger, so to speak, Tony knew he would be indirectly responsible.

Indirectly? I think you're being a bit easy on yourself.

It was true. The suit was his; ergo, the responsibility was his.

With great power . . . and so on and so forth.

And if there was one thing Tony had always hated, it was responsibility.

So better make sure no one dies here today.

It was science for dummies that fire hated water, so Tony's plan was to submerge Vanger until his flames went out, and this worked fine initially.

They collided in the air above the environmental ministers, who did not react as quickly as Tony had hoped. In fact, they smiled and clapped as though this was another part of the show, until their security teams hustled them toward various bulletproof limos parked at various strategic exits.

Tony's momentum bore both suits up and out, through a side pane and over the river. Already Tony could feel how mismatched the contest was. His own suit was lightweight in comparison with the augmented Party Pack. He felt like a monkey wrestling an elephant. All he had going for him was surprise and guile.

They tumbled through the air, Tony punching Vanger as they went. Having a lot more flight hours under his belt than the other man, Tony's reactions were better attuned to in-air combat, and he got in a good dozen strikes before Vanger even realized what was happening. Tony would have liked to have done a little more damage, but he only managed to crack his enemy's chest plate.

'This is great!' enthused Prototony. 'I am loving this. Let that sucker have it, T-Star. Put that bad boy down.'

'Shut up and manipulate my legs,' grunted Tony. 'Put those knee pads to work. And find me a weak spot.'

'Legs and weak spot,' said Prototony, ignoring the fact that he had just been ordered to shut up. The AI set Tony's knees pistoning into Vanger's midsection at a speed that would have utterly pulverized both men's bones had they not been wearing armour.

'Are we fighting?' asked Vanger, once he had control of his wits. ''Cause I can't feel a thing.'

Tony battled on. He knew that the relatively puny force mustered by his engines couldn't do much damage to the souped-up Party Pack, but he didn't see how he had any choice. It was either fight or sit back and watch his creation wipe out some of the most important people in the world.

Keep talking, he thought as he punched. *Let me find that weak spot*.

And there would be a weak spot. Tony Stark knew engineering, and there was no way to attach that many add-ons without overloading a stress point somewhere. The Iron Man suits were marvels of precision construction, arrived at after dozens of prototypes, many of the earlier ones having simply shaken themselves to pieces. The hip bone was connected to the thigh bone, as everybody knew, except with the Iron Man suits there were a thousand hip bones, so to speak, so even the slightest change in repulsor calibration could have catastrophic effects on the suit's system.

They tumbled through the morning sky and into the dark waters of the Liffey, where the pair clunked along the riverbed. Prototony carried out his orders with gusto, and Tony was glad that he couldn't feel anything from the waist down or his life would have been one long scream.

'Is that it?' said Vanger, and he seemed to be enjoying the battle now that he was pretty sure Tony Stark had nothing much in the tank. 'You wanna play tiddledywinks, Stark? Maybe knit a few sweaters for some little dogs?'

This was good material, but Tony did not rejoin. He was too busy worrying about all the alerts suddenly flashing up on his screen.

S UHVVXUHI#R{|J HQI#EDWWHU|I#P P IQHQW#HQJ IQH#DLOXUHI

Come on, P-Tone, he thought, *find me a hole.*

'What would happen if I actually hit you?' wondered Vanger, except he wasn't actually wondering, he was foreshadowing. Without waiting for Tony to respond, he delivered a massive blow to the ambulance suit's solar plexus, sending Tony skidding backwards through the mud, the suit's fingers and toes scraping deep furrows.

'Oooh,' said Prototony, 'that's gotta hurt, T-Star. I am so glad not to be human right now. Even my terabytes are wincing.'

Tony's legs were beginning to ache, and he was more than likely concussed and probably in shock, so he was not capable of making responsible decisions. Which became immediately obvious when he coughed and said:

'Find me a way to take this nutjob down.'

Prototony actually laughed. 'Take him down? It was going good for a few seconds there, but we are done, baby. Lie down and breathe slow till the boat gets here.'

Through the murky water, Tony saw Vanger point a finger.

'Stay there, Stark,' he said, his voice buzzing in Tony's busted earpieces. 'I got a few people to fry, and I'll be right back.'

Without another word, he blasted out of the river into the air above.

It's usually me doing that, thought Tony. Then he asked Prototony, 'Did you find me a hole?'

'Yes and no. I mean, I don't even wanna mention it, because there's nothing you can do.'

'Mention it,' said Tony, routing power to the boots. 'Mention it fast.'

'Okay, take it easy. I found a hole. In fact, I found a hundred, which is what makes it so impossible. The flamethrower's pipework is woven through the suit. Those pipes get super hot super quick, unless they're vented, which they are. Whoever modified the suit hacked vents right out of the armour.'

Stark was miles ahead of him. 'So if I could cover some of the vents, then the suit would be compromised.'

'Compromised to hell and back,' said Prototony.

'But you would have to cover *all* the vents, and the flamethrowers themselves. And I can't see any way to do that.'

'Yes, you can,' said Tony, and he blasted off in Vanger's wake.

The dunking had not affected Vanger's flamethrowers whatsoever. After all, what kind of idiot would fly a mission over water to a rain-sodden country like Ireland without waterproof equipment? *A total idiot* was the answer to that one. Cole Vanger was many things, but a total idiot was not one of them – not when it came to his equipment. Sure, he could fly off the handle at times, had a *fiery* disposition, ha-ha. But when he was inside the storm of action, Vanger was the calmest person in the field. Tussling with Tony Stark underwater might be too much for some people's nerves but not Cole Vanger's. He had a job to do and the equipment to do it. Vanger had confidence, too, in truckloads. He wasn't smug in his abilities. Smug button men didn't tend to last very long in his world. But Vanger was assured and could adapt to changing situations.

Like now, for example. Plan A was obviously a total bust. The environmental ministers had scattered to their cars. But unfortunately for them, the crowd congestion was so severe that there was only one way out of the area: across the Samuel Beckett Bridge. Even as Vanger had been rupturing Stark's innards with a punch, he had been plotting his upwards arc so he would emerge from the river level with the bridge. One sweep of his flamethrowers and he could blow a hole in that bridge bigger than the one in the ozone layer those guys were trying to plug.

Inside the helmet, Vanger smiled. That's how relaxed he was, making jokes and stuff.

Vanger shucked his forearms and the armoured panels peeled back, revealing the pilot lights underneath.

'Time to fry,' he said, which he was considering adopting as his catchphrase, and he sent twin jets of burning liquid and flame surging into the cables over the bridge, enjoying the groans and piano string twangs as they stretched and snapped. He could have simply melted the cars themselves – and he would do that momentarily, just to be sure – but he could not help enjoying one extra blast of beautiful liquid fire.

For a moment he was mesmerized by the dancing flames. He could see little demons writhing inside every blob of melting metal before he blinked and unleashed his flaming jets once more.

Tony surged out of the water in time to see the first jet cut through the cabling. Luckily, Vanger seemed to drift off for a moment; he just hung there rather than finish the job right away, giving Tony's battered suit the second it needed to use the last of its power to draw level with him.

Just as Vanger cut loose with his deadly fuel, Tony closed the fingers of his gloves over Pyro's nozzles and released the Medi-suit's payload of fire extinguisher, which was housed in twin pressure units in the gauntlets and funnelled through the fingertips. The air propellant drove the foam firefighting agent from Tony's fingertips, coating Vanger's flamethrowers and temporarily extinguishing the flames. Furthermore, the foam hardened on contact with the air, forming a seal over the nozzles.

The cars on the bridge were safe – for the moment. And it would be a very short moment, like maybe one Mississippi, two Mississippi, three Mississippi, tops.

Unless Tony Stark had another trick up his sleeve. Which he did. Literally.

'You haven't saved anybody, Stark,' said Vanger. 'I will burn away your pathetic gunk and burn you to a crisp.'

And Tony Stark said, 'Transfer protocol twenty-nine. Personal security override.'

'Twenty-nine?' said Vanger. 'What the hell does that mean?' and even as he asked, the self-proclaimed Pyro was turning up the heat, burning through the shell covering his flamethrowers.

'I wasn't talking to you,' said Tony.

'Transfer protocol twenty-nine?' said Prototony. 'Come on, T-Star. Don't make me do it. I don't wanna be known as the AI who lost the boss.'

'Do it,' said Tony with barely a shake in his voice. 'Do it now.'

So Prototony did as he was told.

Actually, there was only one transfer protocol, not twenty-nine. Tony had named the operation after the length of the longest snake ever verifiably measured, a South American anaconda that tipped the ruler at over twenty-nine feet. The point being nothing to do with the length of the thing per se but the fact that the measurement was taken from an intact shed snakeskin. The point being that in times of necessity, the anaconda could shed its skin. The Medi-suit had a similar protocol in that it could be transferred from one patient to another with extreme rapidity if circumstances dictated. For example, in a multiple-victim scenario where one patient had been stabilized and a second was in critical condition, the Medi-suit was configured to eject patient A and cocoon patient B if it deemed that patient A was in less need of medical treatment than patient B. That was most definitely not the case now, but Tony Stark had overridden the suit's autonomy with his own voice, so Prototony had no option but to obey.

The Medi-suit made a noise that could only be described as a *whang* as every plate in the suit reversed itself and crawled up Vanger's frame, completely encasing his own suit, seals stretching to cover the extra bulk. Cole Vanger did not even have time to realize what was happening before his weight increased drastically and his every vent was blocked.

Tony's plan was simple. Vanger was now too heavy to fly and his nozzles were permanently closed off, so the double-plated suit would simply send him sinking like a stone to the bottom of the river until harbour police could get some divers down there.

'Give it up, Vanger,' Tony shouted into Pyro's faceplate. 'You're done here.' And then he could hold on no longer and fell back toward the freezing water, satisfied – as much as he could feel satisfaction in his bashed-up state – that he had saved many lives and not taken a single one.

But what Tony didn't know and couldn't know was that Vanger had made some modifications to the suit that seemed like a good idea at the time but were about to make him rather hot under the collar.

The vents that Vanger had cut into the Party Pack were to be his undoing. These openings were not part of the original Iron Man schematics and therefore did not show up on any systems check. So Vanger, oblivious to the danger, fired ahead gung ho with his pressure build, convinced that his only option was to unleash hellfire and scorch through whatever was blocking his pipes. Unfortunately for him, his nozzles still had gunk in the tubes and his cooling and pressure vents were completely encased in a second skin of armour, so the Party Pack quickly grew hotter than any party should ever be. In fact, in less than ten seconds the temperature rose at such a screaming rate that the entire jerry-rigged flamethrowing apparatus virtually ate itself and exploded, which at that point was a relief for poor Cole Vanger, who at the very end realized he was not as fond of flames as he had thought.

It was not smooth sailing for Tony Stark, either. He was ejected from the back of the suit twenty feet over the slate-coloured water, with little in the way of insulation other than some retro-trendy sports gear and inflatable leg casts. In the ten seconds it took poor unfortunate Cole Vanger to superheat, Tony dropped into the ocean with a remarkable lack of elegance for one who was usually so coordinated. One unkind reporter would later describe his tumble as a 'fall from grace,' which would make Rhodey almost bust a gut laughing when he saw the meme. Then Tony would take offence and they'd wrestle and knock over a costly Guggi brass-rimmed bowl. But Tony was not thinking about taking offence during the fall; he was realizing that he had never seen his own butt from that angle before and maybe he should do a few glute exercises if he survived. Then he was in the water, watching semiconscious as Vanger went supernova overhead and groggily thinking, *Pretty colours,* before the icy temperature shocked him alert and the thigh-high leg casts bobbed him up to the surface.

So no, it was not smooth sailing for Tony Stark. It was more like smooth floating.

Tony lay there for a few moments, savouring not being dead and ignoring the hundreds of Iron Man fans shooting photos of him from shore.

One rangy blond man jogged to the centre of the

bridge while everyone else was racing off. He hung over the railing, which was sagging dangerously, and pointed the funnel of a bullhorn at Tony.

'Mr Stark, is it yourself?'

Tony was not sure how to answer this question. 'Ah ... yes. I am myself.'

'I thought as much, unless you were someone else, which you were earlier, by the way. Inspector Conroy here. Irish security service. I suppose you could say that between the pair of us, we saved the day.'

Tony chuckled and it sent waves of pain travelling down his legs.

'I suppose you could say that.'

'That other fellow who was you before, he was a bit moody, wasn't he? With all the *whooshing* and what have you.'

'Moody. That's one word for him. And he certainly did like his *whooshing*.'

'And I'll tell you another thing,' continued Conroy. 'You're a brave man, taking a dip in that water. Sure the bacteria in there is off the charts. You'll have it coming out of both ends for weeks.'

Tony realized that Ireland was quite different from other countries, and he found he liked this Conroy person instinctively, even though they were carrying on a normal conversation in the middle of this most abnormal set of circumstances. He also saw how the inspector was taking stock of the situation and speaking tersely into a radio while also chatting with Tony, and he thought that maybe this guy was a whole lot sharper than his chit-chat suggested.

'You do see that my legs are broken, Inspector?'

Conroy winced. 'I saw that, all right. More bends on them than old winter twigs. I was distracting you – that's a technique, you know. Hostage negotiators love that one. Can't get enough of it. Magicians, too. Like that Blaine fella.'

'You're doing it again, right?'

'Right you are, Mr Stark. Let's just me and you have a little chinwag until the lifeboat gets here. Couple of minutes is all.'

Tony thought that a little "chinwag" with the charming inspector would be quite delightful, and then he remembered that this affair was far from over.

He coughed, clearing the remaining water from his throat, and asked quietly, 'Prototony, you still in there, or did you hightail it back to base?'

The question was picked up by the built-in microphone in Tony's earpiece.

'Still in your ear, T-Star,' said the AI. 'You know P-Tone wouldn't abandon you unless absolutely necessary.'

'How far away is the yacht?'

'I've already called her in. Two minutes, max.'

'Good. Order more painkillers. And coffee. And some thermal underwear. Maybe a cheeseburger.'

'Okay, boss. Anything else?'

Tony thought of the Mandarin, who had caused all this mayhem, and he shivered with cold and rage.

'Yeah. Switch on the 3-D printer. I need some new hardware.'

The whistle of Conroy's bullhorn took Tony's attention away from his own ear.

'Who are you talking to there, Tony boy?' asked the inspector. 'Hearing voices, are you? I'd say that's the pain. Pain makes a man hear and see strange things. I broke my nose once and I thought I saw the Road Runner. And sure that fella's a cartoon character.'

Tony smiled. 'I want that guy on the payroll,' he said to Prototony. 'I could listen to him all day.'

'But not today, T-Star?'

'No, not today,' said Tony, thinking now about Saoirse. He had left her at the Mandarin's mercy – not that he'd had any choice, but that didn't make him feel any better about it. 'I'm on a mission today.'

'What kind of mission?'

Tony flicked his eyes sideways to see the *Tanngrisnir* slicing through the water on automatic pilot.

'I'm not sure yet,' he said grimly. 'Either rescue or revenge.'

Seventy seconds later, the Stark yacht drew alongside its owner, dipped a robotic scoop into the river, and bore the billionaire playboy philanthropist towards Dublin Bay.

'Would you look at that?' said Conroy to no one in particular. 'The fella has an enormous scoop on his yacht. Money to burn, I suppose.' Conroy was halfway to shore before it occurred to him that he had possibly asked the wrong Tony for Taylor Swift's contact details.

'Chance missed, Inspector,' he admonished himself. 'Golden opportunity shaken off.'

Then something else occurred to him: if he let Tony Stark sail out of this complicated situation, the higher-ups would have his guts for neckties.

'Hold on there now, Tony boy,' he called, running back towards the yacht. 'I know we're friends and so forth, but there are serious questions to answer here. Like how come one of your suits just attacked the convention centre?'

At this point the beleaguered bridge sagged alarmingly and the cables rippled like jump ropes, and Inspector Conroy found himself alone on a bridge that was about to collapse into the River Liffey.

Diavolo, boy, he thought, *this is one of those sticky situations you were trained for. Some quick thinking is called for.*

Diavolo Conroy's mother had often repeated the old chestnut, 'Up here for thinking, Diavolo,' pointing at her head, 'and down there for dancing,' pointing at her feet. Conroy had always thought she was stating the obvious, but right now he could see that it was a time for dancing rather than thinking. His feet took on a mind of their own and danced him between the raining blobs of molten metal and around the fallen cables and down the sloping walkway that had dipped to such an extent that it more or less formed a gangway for Conroy to step onto the roof of the *Tanngrisnir*'s forward cabin.

It was such a bizarre way to escape deadly danger

that Diavolo Conroy could barely believe it had actually happened.

'You're probably in shock, so you are,' he said to himself, and then he smoothed back his sandy hair and climbed down a ladder to the main deck. Just in time, as it turned out, for if he had still been up top when Tony Stark opened the throttle, he would have been blown off the roof like an insect.

THE CONTINGENCY PLAN

On board the Mandarin's boat, the mood was grim to say the least. The only permitted communication with the outside world was an old rabbit-eared television tuned to an Irish news channel. And while the news was riveting, it certainly was not the news the Mandarin and his shrinking crew had been hoping for.

The Mandarin permitted himself an explosive moment of rage, punching a hole in the television screen and causing quite an impressive shower of sparks and a minor explosion.

'The devil take you, Tony Stark,' he said, and his crew shrank back against the galley walls, moving themselves out of arm's reach.

Spin Zhuk did not shrink far enough, and the Mandarin

pinned her against the refrigerator, his fingers encircling her neck.

'The girl is dead?' he said.

'Yes, chef,' said Spin. 'One shot. You heard it.'

'We all heard a shot, but you know the procedure. A kill must be confirmed by photographic evidence. You produced no photograph.'

'She was just a child, and I did not consider her a threat.'

The Mandarin's fingers tightened. 'This girl hacked Iron Man, and you did not consider her a threat?'

Spin's voice rasped on the way out. 'And anyway, the waves were taking her, and her head was blown almost clean off. I swear it, chef.'

The Mandarin stared deep into Zhuk's eyes and the Ukrainian driver could swear that her memories were an open book to this man. His green-eyed gaze seemed to bore into her and fillet the truth from her lies. But eventually, he released her neck and stroked her trembling cheek.

'But of course, Spin. My dear Spin. You have always been my most loyal soldier. You have never let me down. I am – what is the word? – *testy*. Yes, that is it. Testy. We must proceed without Mr Vanger.'

'You are speaking of plan B,' said Freddie Leveque.

The Mandarin whirled on him. 'No, Freddie. The term *plan B* implies some inferiority in the strategy. I prefer to call it our contingency plan. We know from our sources that five of the seven ministers will stay at the luxury golf estate, the Royal G. This is where we will strike. The attack will not be so public, but at least my reputation will be mostly intact, as will our mission. The other two ministers – Russia and Argentina, I believe – can be picked off at a later date. Freddie, you will enjoy this responsibility.'

'I will enjoy zis,' said Leveque.

The Mandarin frowned. 'In the name of heaven, Freddie, learn to pronounce your T-Hs. You are almost forty years old. I will give you two weeks; after that there will be consequences.'

Leveque's face lost its usual cocky grin. He was already on shaky ground, having been outfoxed by Tony Stark, and now the chef was taking issue with his pronunciation.

'Of course, chef. I will do zis … dis … this *immédiatement*.'

'Very well,' said the Mandarin, seemingly mollified. 'I thank you, and my ears thank you. And now, it seems obvious that Mr Vanger will not be coming back, so take us out, Miss Zhuk.'

'Yes, chef. Out we shall go.'

'Full stealth every inch of the way. Low speed and no jets. If a fisherman sees us, I want him to think we are a breaching whale. There is plenty of time.'

'Yes, zere is time,' said Leveque, and then, '*There* is time. *Mon dieu*, *this* will be difficult.'

'Yes, indeed,' said the Mandarin. 'But a lot less

difficult than eating with your mouth sewn shut, eh, *mon ami*?'

Leveque instinctively pawed at his lips to ensure they had not already been sewn shut, then simply nodded his understanding, unwilling to risk another sentence. The Mandarin did not make specific threats lightly. Freddie Leveque had personally witnessed him knocking a person's block off. It had taken him three swings with a sledgehammer, but he had managed it. Leveque would never forget the chef's comment when the job was done.

'I am surprised,' the Mandarin had said, slightly bemused. 'I had assumed "knocking someone's block off" to be a figure of speech, but it seems to have its roots in reality. Impractical, certainly, but possible. Interesting, *n'est-ce pas*, Freddie?'

And even Freddie Leveque, who was known for his quick temper and violent outbursts, had been shocked.

So when the Mandarin threatened to sew Leveque's mouth shut, Freddie was absolutely certain he would do it, even over something as trivial as bad pronunciation. And Leveque was equally certain that there would be no anaesthetic involved.

When Spin Zhuk had sworn to her boss that the waves had taken Saoirse Tory's body, the wheelwoman had been lying, as far as she knew. But in actuality there was some truth to her words, for the waves *had* borne Saoirse's body away, inasmuch as they had carried off the Mandarin's stealth gunboat, in which Saoirse was now hiding.

And why in the name of heaven and all other postmortal states would the Irish girl hide out on the craft of a ruthless assassin who had often reiterated his desire to see her dead at the very least?

Here follows the logic: Saoirse reasoned that the Mandarin and his troops would scour the island looking for her, but they would never think to search their own boat. After all, what kind of lunatic would hide out inside the mouth of a shark, so to speak? Also, there was the chance that she could steal the boat and leave the entire bunch on the island to be rounded up by the authorities.

So when the blowholes temporarily dislodged Spin Zhuk from the earth, Saoirse ducked into a ravine and skipped through the familiar shadows, flanking her bamboozled would-be captor. With every step the familiar crags bolstered her confidence, and the ghost of her grandfather guided her path.

Twenty-eight seconds, girl. You snatched my record. Watch your feet now. There's dark weed on that rock. And up there, to your left, a handhold. Remember? I showed you that on the day you lost your knife to the ocean.

Even imagining her grandfather was enough to soothe Saoirse's fevered mind.

I could stay down here, she realized, *in the network of ravines, and they would never find me.*

It had been her grandfather who had taken the young Saoirse off for long summer days hiking the island, exploring the drumlins and gullies, watching the pollack bump their noses against the harbour wall and the tiny crabs scuttle around on the seabed like harried business people on their way to work. It had been her grandfather, too, the mariner, who had told her about Fourni and the struggles of the people in their daily lives. Because of Granddad Francis she had involved her entire school in fund-raising to build the orphanage in Port Verdé. Because of her grandfather she had designed the translator app that had paid for most of the project. Because of him she had visited Port Verdé herself and met the young girls who had been helped by her school's efforts. And because of her efforts she had known her grandfather was proud of her before he died.

So no, she would not hide in the gullies.

The man she had known as Joseph Chen had tricked her. He had made her an accomplice to murder, and she would stop him or die trying. Which was why Saoirse Tory chose to abandon the trails and hidey-holes of her younger days and re-enter the fray.

The gunboat, she thought. *Perhaps I can radio the coast guard. And if I can steal the craft, then the Mandarin will be stranded on Little Saltee until the authorities arrive.*

The boat was an unfamiliar model, but Saoirse had been around seafarers all her life and was pretty confident she could figure out the controls.

After all, she thought, *I flew the Iron Man suit.*

With this daring – and some might fairly say insane

– plan in mind, Saoirse took the moral high road, which was the actual low road that led through the granite crags to the small harbour hewn by medieval chisels from the solid rock.

Her determination was almost derailed by the sound of a single shot that she for an instant thought was aimed at her, but she quickly realized that Spin Zhuk must be signaling to the others that she had escaped.

Time is ticking on, Saoirse girl, said her granddad in her ear. *Those fellas will be coming 'round the mountain any second. If you're set on this plan, then make your move.*

To which the ghost of Tony Stark added, *Yeah, Friday. Let's see what you've got under the hood.*

So Saoirse left the cover of the rocks and sprinted down the short pier, thinking, *Now Stark's in* my *head? I suppose turnaround is fair play, as Granddad always said.*

The gunship seemed unguarded, and in all honesty it did not seem much like a gunship. Freddie Leveque had pronounced it *gunsheep* in his French accent, which Saoirse thought now was appropriate.

A wolf in gunsheep's clothing. Ha-ha.

At first glance the gunship appeared to be nothing more sinister than a large fishing trawler, which was only sinister if you happened to be a fish. It wasn't factory-ship big, maybe fifty feet from stem to stern with a sleek profile for a work vessel, but nothing too unusual – until one looked a little closer and realized the hull was reinforced with armoured plating and the cabin roof bristled with enough porcupine-quill antennae to hack the CIA, which they had, twice.

For now the boat was unguarded, though Saoirse knew it would not be for long, so she would have to jump through this window of opportunity while it was open a crack.

She jumped through the metaphorical window, which was an actual door, and was relieved a second time to find no one on the bridge. She hopped onto the stool by the main control panel and ratcheted it up until she was level with the console.

'Moron,' she said to the console, which wasn't fair, because the console was definitely not a moron. In fact, it was a high-tech surveillance and navigation system with two-thousand-bit encryption, which was virtually unbreakable. But as far as Saoirse was concerned, the key word was *virtually*.

Iron Man was considered absolutely secure, and I broke into that system.

And perhaps Saoirse would have managed it – she certainly had the smarts – but she was outfoxed by the thumbprint scanner on the power button that would wake the computers from sleep. That and the sound of footsteps on the dock.

The Mandarin! she realized and jumped from the stool. Nothing to do now but hide, and that seemed so childish, so stupid that it could never work.

All the brains in the world, and all I can think to do is hide.

Let me tell you, Saoirse girl, said the ghost of her granddad, *hiding beats dying every minute of the day and every day of the week.*

Amen, brother, said Tony Stark, who was getting very pally with her granddad all of a sudden.

But they were both right, Saoirse knew. There was nothing to do but hide.

She turned and scanned the bridge desperately for somewhere to stash herself – somewhere that might not be examined too closely.

Her eyes landed on the stowage cabinet above the semicircular couch area on the port side. This was where the life jackets were traditionally kept. It would be a tight squeeze, certainly, but possibly a spot that would remain unchecked – and if the ship went down, at least she would have a life jacket.

Saoirse opened the nearest cabinet door, then bounced a couple of times on the sofa until she had the altitude to get a grip on the bottom of the shelf. She hoisted herself up, wriggled inside, and nestled between the life jackets and sacks of junk. It was only when the Mandarin and his remaining warriors trooped onto the bridge that Saoirse remembered something.

I forgot to reset the stool.

Which would be a really stupid reason to get killed.

Saoirse lay zigzagged in the storage cabinet, her body folded between the life jackets and seafaring detritus, waiting to be discovered and shot, which was not quite as cheery as waiting for Santa. Squinting through a crack in the door, she witnessed the Mandarin punch the television set, and she knew then that Tony Stark was alive and Cole Vanger had died in his attempt to assassinate the environmental ministers.

In your fat lying face, Chen, or whatever your name is! she exulted internally, and then, *Go, Tony, you egotistical capitalist.*

Once the exulting fever had passed, Saoirse got back to the business of staying alive, which mostly involved shallow breathing, ignoring itches and resisting the impulse to cry out, 'You idiots betrayed me!'

She lay there and discovered that Spin Zhuk was claiming to have shot her. It crossed her mind that she should reveal herself just to get Spin in trouble, but this notion was as fleeting as it was idiotic, and Saoirse decided that she would keep up her shallow-breathing routine rather than get herself tossed overboard to prove a point.

Her only sticky moment came when, moments later, Spin was left alone on the bridge and set about plotting the course to the small inlet north of Dublin city in which the Royal G nestled. Without looking at the stool, Spin pointed her own seat at its seat – or rather, where its seat should have been – but instead, she got bumped in the small of her back.

'Huh?' she said thoughtfully, spinning the seat on its

swivel. 'I am not leaving it this way.'

Inside the storage cabinet, Saoirse quailed and stopped breathing altogether, hugging a random sack of junk.

But Spin Zhuk's mind supplied an explanation for itself. 'Stupid Leveque,' she said, 'and his stupid little legs. Always he messes with my settings.' And she tugged at the adjustment lever until the seat dropped to her liking.

Saoirse allowed herself a relieved exhale, but it was a quiet one, as though she were warming her hands, and she hugged the sack closer for comfort. Something about the contours of whatever was inside seemed familiar.

'No way,' she whispered, or more accurately, she made the shapes of the words with her mouth.

If what was inside the sack was what she thought was inside, then she might have found a way to contact Tony Stark.

Tony Stark would not have been much use to Saoirse at that moment even if she had been able to contact him. He was lying on the operating table in his yacht's sick bay, having both his legs operated on by robot arms that moved at dazzling speeds inside a blob of clear gel that covered Stark to his neck.

Diavolo Conroy was watching the process with less amazement than might be expected under the circumstances.

'I'm guessing, Tony boy,' said the Irish inspector, 'that this treatment is not available on Medicare?'

'And I'm guessing that your parents liked pizza, to

name you Diavolo,' said Tony.

'It's a long story,' said Diavolo, 'which normally I would love to tell you, but there are more pressing matters. Like those robots with lasers. Do they know what they're doing?'

'Pretty much,' said Tony. 'Still a few bugs to iron out.'

As if to prove his point, a robot arm sliced off one of Stark's little toes, then hurriedly lasered it back on.

'Holy mother of baby leprechauns,' exclaimed Conroy.

Stark had felt not a thing. 'What happened?'

The robot arm at fault seemed to wink its laser eye at Conroy, asking him to keep this little misstep between them. 'Nothing, Tony. I'm just amazed at your genius, that's all.'

Tony Stark had no problem accepting this. 'I know. I'm a bit of a stunner in the mind field. This gel, for example, is made mostly from the excretions of a certain type of South American worm. Amazing healing-acceleration qualities.'

'Magic worms, is it?' said Conroy doubtfully. 'Would you be on some kind of medication, by any chance?'

Stark laughed. 'It's hard to accept, I know. But the secrets to life are in the rainforests, and we're hacking them to death.'

Conroy poked the gel, watching the ripples spawn across its surface. His pal the robot arm shot him an evil laser glare and he hurriedly withdrew his finger.

'Careful there, Inspector,' said Stark. 'You don't

wanna introduce any contaminants to this environment or your hand is likely to get cut off.'

Conroy thought back to the previous minute's toe amputation. 'You have no idea, Tony boy.'

'Actually, you might want to step outside; this next part isn't going to be pretty. Thing One and Thing Two are going to slice open my legs and glue the bones together. No time to wait for nature to take its course.'

Conroy laughed. 'Thing One and Thing Two? You named your robot doctors after Dr Seuss characters?'

'Yeah. I learned everything I know about human nature from *The Cat in the Hat*.'

'I got most of my life lessons from *The Hobbit*,' admitted Diavolo Conroy.

'So are you going outside?'

'I thought I might record your operation,' said Conroy. 'A fella would get a fair amount of likes from that kind of a video.'

'Your phone won't work in here,' Tony told him. 'Static is all you'll get. We're running dark.'

Conroy worked in a nice segue. 'Static? You have no idea the static I'll get back in the office. I am supposed to be bringing you in for questioning, not gallivanting around the high seas.'

'First, we're not gallivanting. We are hunting down an assassin and his captive.'

'First? So what's second?'

'Second,' said Stark, smiling in spite of his contusions

and breaks. 'Second, nice segue. I appreciate the effort.'

'You're welcome,' said Conroy. 'And now if you don't mind, I think I will step up on deck.'

The Irish inspector had grown up gutting fish after school and so had a strong stomach, but the combination of the thrumming engines and the sight of laser arms slicing through a man's flesh was enough to generate a little queasiness in anyone.

'Okay, Inspector,' said Tony. 'Don't fall overboard.'

Conroy smiled. 'Sure and if I do, your big scoop yoke will swing down and rescue me, isn't that right?'

Below Stark's eye line, Thing 1 and Thing 2 were busy cutting and pasting his legs, working so fast that the worm gel rippled. Tony obviously could not feel any pain. 'Not unless I tell it to,' he said.

'Well then, Tony boy,' said Diavolo Conroy, 'don't fall asleep so.'

Once Spin Zhuk had programmed a course, she slipped on a set of headphones and turned up AC/DC so loud that Saoirse could make out the tinny tune from where she was hiding.

Thanks, Spin, she thought. *That gives me a little wiggle room to investigate what's in the bag.*

In fact she had very little actual wiggle room, as the space was built to contain whatever needed to be stored within easy reach of the control console and not to stow away teenagers with a grudge.

A legitimate grudge, thought Saoirse. *The Mandarin tried to make me an accessory to mass murder.*

Saoirse had always thought herself to be the smartest person in the room, but now she was realizing that there were different kinds of smart. She was a science genius, but the Mandarin was a master manipulator and had made it seem like she was recruiting him when in fact he was ensnaring her, making her an unwitting member of his murderous team.

And even if I do somehow get my revenge on him, Liz and her orphans are still in the hands of a gang of hoodlums.

This particular thought threatened to drive Saoirse to the edge of crazy, so she decided to shut it away for the time being.

One seemingly insurmountable problem at a time, she told herself. *But I haven't forgotten you, Liz.*

For now she needed to confirm that what she thought was in the bag was actually in the bag.

Saoirse inched onto her side and felt around the heavy canvas until she located a zipper. She traced the zipper to its end, where her fingers found the slider, and then she tugged oh so carefully – tooth by tooth in fact – so as not to alert Spin Zhuk with a sharp series of clicks, which was just the type of noise that might penetrate the heavy-metal music.

Saoirse slid her hand inside the bag and felt something smooth and metallic, maybe the size of a large melon.

Encouraging.

Her suspicions were confirmed when her fingers slid into two rectangular eyeholes.

'Hello, there,' she whispered, gently easing the Party Pack's Iron Man helmet from the bag. It was cold and dead in her hands without a power source to run its systems, but Saoirse happened to know that the entire helmet was an induction smart plate that could drain power from almost any source, provided a person knew how to activate the system.

As I do, thought Saoirse.

She wiggled a finger underneath the jaw plate and pressed the UHOHDVH button. All she needed to do was get the helmet within six inches of a power source. The closer the helmet, the quicker the charge.

Saoirse slid her head inside the helmet and tightened the seal around her throat. Wearing the helmet gave her the advantage of motion and thermal sensors, not to mention the possibility of getting a message out to Stark. She was now effectively soundproofed, but she would not test that out by laughing hysterically or indeed shouting abuse at Spin Zhuk. She would save her words for when they were absolutely necessary.

She cleared a path for her head until the helmet clunked softly against a power cable that was threaded through the rear of the cabinet. Within seconds a battery symbol glowed softly – a solitary icon on an otherwise dead display.

My North Star, thought Saoirse. *You might not lead me*

home, but you will lead Stark to me.

Nothing to do now but lie there in absolute silence, let the helmet suck juice from the boat's batteries, and pray no one noticed the power drain. Pray, too, that none of her bodily functions betrayed her, for a tummy gurgle could prove fatal if Spin Zhuk turned down her tunes.

Come on, Iron Man, she urged the helmet. *Wake up and send me a hero.*

Was she really thinking of arrogant billionaire Tony Stark as a hero now?

Well, perhaps not a hero exactly, but he had stopped Vanger in his flaming tracks, so there was potential.

HINTS AND RIDDLES

The *Tanngrisnir*

Tony was floating in an anaesthetic-induced stupor, half dreaming and half-awake. And in that in-between place, his father came to him, looking as handsome as Tony remembered – aside from his eyes, which were all white. Tony knew he was dreaming and so was not alarmed by the creepy eyes. He was, however, interested in what his subconscious was trying to tell him.

'Dad,' he said, 'what's up?'

'Not you,' said his father. 'You are certainly not up. This Mandarin character has brought you low.'

'Yeah,' admitted Tony. 'You got me there. But you should see the other guy, Vanger.'

'Oh, I am seeing him,' said Howard Stark. 'He's here

now, trying to reassemble his parts. Another body on the Stark ledger.'

'No fair, Dad. He did that to himself. I saved a lot of people.'

Howard shrugged and his white eyes flashed. 'Saved, killed. It's the business you're in.'

'*Your* business,' argued Tony.

Howard closed his eyes, and for a moment those spooky white lights were shuttered. 'I know, Son. I've had time to reflect. You were right. Absolutely right about everything. Duran Duran is a great band, and your hair always did look fabulous. What's more, you've always made your mother and me so proud.'

Tony was not falling for this. 'You need to do better than that, subconscious. My father was not in the business of handing out compliments.'

'You got me,' said Howard. 'I was just telling you what you've always wanted to hear.'

At one time this would have made Tony so happy, but now he needed more.

'What about some insight? A few nuggets of wisdom from the afterlife?'

Howard blinked and the white lights strobed. 'That's more difficult. We're only allowed to give vague hints and riddles.'

'Tell me what I'm supposed to do. I've been trying to clean up our family mess.'

'Do you remember what I said about toys?'

'Are you kidding? I'll never forget.' Tony cleared his throat and put on his father's deep voice and old-timey 1950s Noo Yawk accent. *'There are no toys in this world, just unevolved weapons.'*

'In a nutshell, yes. And now here comes the riddle part. Listen closely, Son.'

'Great,' said Tony. 'Vagueness and riddles. I think I liked it better when you ignored me.'

Howard turned the high beams of his eye lights directly on Tony and said:

> 'Turnaround is fair play.
> What once was left
> Is right today.
> It is not enough
> To fill the hole.
> But climb the hill
> To win your soul.'

Tony moaned. 'Come on, Dad. That's fortune cookie gibberish. We're Starks. We don't deal in abstracts. I've got stuff to do. Life-and-death business. Couldn't you just spell it out for me?'

Howard Stark sighed. 'Tony, you need to get a little culture in your life.'

'Dad, a hint, please. What hole? Is that a real hole somewhere? Or like, a metaphorical hole?'

'Very well, my son. I shall give you a clue.

Listen closely.'

'Now you're talking.'

'The hole of which I speak is actually … a signal. We have a signal.'

This didn't help Tony one bit. 'That's worse than the riddle. What do you mean we have a signal?'

Howard opened his eyes wide and blinding light filled Tony's dream. 'I mean we have a signal. Someone is trying to get in touch.'

Tony knew somehow that his dream or vision or whatever was coming to an end. He had never seen his father in this way before and somehow knew that he wouldn't again.

'Dad, wait, please.'

But Howard Stark was lost in the light and only his fading voice lingered. 'Your mother says eat a sandwich, for heaven's sake; you seem thin. And I say grow a real beard. You look like a backstreet loan shark.'

And then Howard Stark was utterly gone, leaving Tony Stark alone, as he had been for so long.

Tony opened his eyes to find himself in the *Tanngrisnir*'s sick bay. He was surprised to find that the dream did not fade like his dreams usually did but stayed in sharp focus.

Later, he thought, *I'll build a Freud avatar and analyze myself. But for now …*

For now, the Mandarin was still out there.

Diavolo Conroy was standing by the bed, looking

down on Stark as though he were a zoo exhibit.

'Look who's awake,' said the Irish inspector. 'The man himself. Robot boy.'

Stark cleared his dry throat. 'Did you say something about a signal?'

'I did,' said Conroy. 'And you called me Dad. I'm flattered and so forth. The wife and I would love to have a child, but I'd prefer one who was somewhat shorter and not quite so willful.'

'Tell me about the signal, Inspector,' insisted Tony.

'Ah, yes. Well, it's probably a malfunction of some sort. I don't have to tell you about malfunctions, what with the toe amputation and all that.'

'What toe amputation?'

Conroy coughed into his hand. 'Nothing. It's an old Irish saying, as in: "Sure you couldn't be up to that fellow and his toe amputations." Its meaning is lost in the mists of time.'

'The signal?'

'Yes, of course. Well, the computer keeps trumpeting that you have a signal on the emergency frequency.'

'From whom?'

'That's the thing,' said Diavolo, sweeping back a lock of blond hair from his face. 'The computer said the signal is coming from your own head.'

Tony threw back the blanket covering him and struggled onto his elbows.

'My own head . . . ' he said. 'She cracked the induction

and is drawing me in.'

Conroy grimaced. 'I know you're some class of a genius, Stark, but not one word of that made a lick of sense.'

Tony grabbed Conroy's shoulder for support, dragging himself out of bed. His legs felt like they belonged to somebody else and he walked a few staggering Frankenstein's monster steps, but at least he didn't collapse.

'What I need to do is see what the printer's got in the basket,' he said to the mystified Conroy. 'And you need to pilot the boat. Can you do that to save a young girl's life?'

'Can I pilot the boat?' said Conroy, fake miffed. 'I'm from the island of Ireland. I was born piloting boats. And I'll pilot this one to the moon and back to save a life. But if you're taking advantage of my good nature, then I'll pilot you straight into a special sitting of the European court.'

'That was a long-winded answer,' said Tony. 'Can you try to be more succinct?'

'I'll make you a deal,' replied Diavolo Conroy. 'I'll keep it short and sweet if you don't call me Dad again.'

'Deal,' said Tony.

YELP + LAUGH = YELPH

The universe has certain rules. Among them are:

He who owns a sharp tool will eventually cut himself.

And:

Laboratory accidents never result in super-hero-type powers.

And most applicable in this case:

He who laughs first gets caught.

The first rule could be, at a stretch, applied to Tony Stark and the Iron Man suit, considering recent events.

One notable exception to the second rule was currently swinging around New York City on spider webs, which did not bear thinking about.

But unfortunately for Saoirse Tory, the last rule was to hold firm – in this case, *she* who laughs first.

*

It happened like this:

Saoirse's head had been stuck inside the helmet for over three hours while she waited for the system to show some sign of life. Up to that point, there had not been so much as a welcome bong, so in spite of the inherent tension of her situation, Saoirse – stressed, dehydrated and exhausted – found herself drifting off to sleep. As a result, when the helmet had leeched enough power from the gunship to reboot, Saoirse was startled and delighted by the sudden appearance of the heads-up display, and she let out a sound that was somewhere between a triumphant laugh and a yelp. This is a sound so common in Australia, where nature is so weird and wonderful that people are always being surprised and delighted, that they even have a name for it. Down Under, that sound is called a *yelph*, which only makes sense phonetically.

So Saoirse yelphed, and unfortunately for her, she did it during those two seconds between metal tracks when Spin Zhuk's ears were actually attuned to the world beyond her headphones. And even more unfortunately, the helmet's seal that Saoirse believed would soundproof her headspace had been calibrated for Tony Stark's thicker neck, so a few decibels of her squeaky exclamation slipped out under the seal and into Spin Zhuk's ears. And to compound the yelph, one of her army boots scraped a wooden door panel.

Spin whipped off her headphones and swivelled on the stool.

'What is this?' she said to herself. 'I am hearing unusual noise.'

Her first thought was *rats*. Even though the Mandarin's gunboat was kept spotlessly clean, she had found the Irish rats to be a tenacious bunch and also somewhat arrogant, often standing their ground when she approached and cheekily twitching their whiskers as if to say, *I'm a rat. I'm here. What are you going to do about it?*

Usually, Spin let her boots do the walking and the talking, but in this case, if there was a rat in the cupboard, then it would be too high up to stomp, and the Mandarin would not approve of her shooting up his storage space. This is why Spin started speaking; she hoped the rat would hear her and scurry off someplace where she wouldn't have to deal with it. She was not overly fond of rats.

'I am coming in your direction, Mr Vermin Rat. So if I was being you, I would pitter-patter away before I reach the door.'

Inside the storage space, the Iron Man helmet's motion sensors were automatically activated, picking up Spin's sudden movement even through the plywood door, and Saoirse found that she could see and hear with greater detail and clarity than ever before. What she could see and hear was a Ukrainian superdriver approaching her hiding place and apparently calling her Mr Vermin Rat.

Saoirse Tory had a prodigious intellect, but she doubted that even Albert Einstein could have come up with a plan in the few seconds allowed her. And the helmet had far from sufficient power to do much more than send out a ping and operate basic sensors.

I am done for, she thought. *Help me, Granddad.*

But the usually chatty spirit of her grandfather had no advice to offer, and Saoirse realized she was completely on her own.

'Run away, Mr Ratty Rat,' said Spin Zhuk. 'Don't make me do the wringing of your furry neck. I will do it without fearing the infection, because there is antibacterial gel in the restroom.'

Spin doesn't like rats, Saoirse realized, though it was no great thunderbolt of knowledge. After all, not many people did. Saoirse herself didn't mind rats, but she hated mackerel, with their evil blue scales and the filmy membrane over their eyes.

Saoirse did not consciously form a strategy, but she saw the fingers of her left hand reach out and scratch the inside of the door.

Fingers! she thought. *What are you doing?*

However, Saoirse may have prematurely scolded her fingers, for Spin Zhuk stopped in her tracks.

'I hear you, Mr Vermin Rat. I am coming.'

But she wasn't coming. Spin Zhuk was walking in place so the rat would think she was coming – something a person probably wouldn't do if she knew another human was watching.

That is so weird, thought the girl in the cupboard pretending to be a rat, and then she kept scratching.

Spin Zhuk scowled at the storage space, visualizing a cocky rat Irish-dancing inside there. Mocking her. Taunting her. Belittling her heritage.

'I am not afraid of you, rat!'

No more 'Mr,' thought Saoirse. *The time for formalities is passed.*

'I am Spin Zhuk and I have fought hungry bears, so I am not afraid of a rat!'

She drew her Sig Sauer from the holster on her shoulder.

For a moment Saoirse was so scared that she forgot to scratch, but then she set two hands to the task, mimicking a couple of rats.

But Spin was set on her course of action now and, with barely a tremble in her gun-free hand, reached up and yanked open the cupboard, hardly giving Saoirse time to pull back her hands and tuck them out of sight, as if that would do any good.

'Aha!' said Spin, then immediately sighed in relief.

Obviously, I am not as scary as a rat or two, thought Saoirse, but then to her surprise Spin proceeded to say:

'Nothing. There is nothing. Just a stupid helmet rolling around.'

Nothing? thought Saoirse. *I may not be a rat, but I am something.*

It took Saoirse a moment to realize what was going on.

All she sees are some life jackets and an empty helmet. Spin thinks the helmet rolled out of the bag.

It was enough to make a near-hysterical person laugh.

And why not? The helmet is soundproofed, and all Spin heard was my boot scraping the panel.

So as Spin Zhuk reached up to close the storage compartment door, Saoirse did laugh, and also said:

'"Nothing. There is nothing. Just a stupid helmet rolling around." *You're* a stupid helmet, Spin.'

Which made no sense, but in fairness to her, Saoirse was under considerable stress.

Spin froze.

'I am knowing this voice,' she said.

'What voice?' asked Saoirse automatically.

'That voice!'

Inside the helmet, Saoirse turned pale. 'You can hear me?'

'Yes, but you are supposed to be dead.'

'I *am* dead,' said Saoirse, not quite able to believe the words coming out of her mouth. 'This is your conscience talking. You will be visited by three spirits.'

This nonsense snapped Spin Zhuk out of whatever rat-phobia fugue she had been in, and she reached inside the compartment and dragged Saoirse kicking and screaming out of her hiding place.

'Silence, child,' said Spin, 'because I must be killing you quietly. Over the side with you. It would be better if you went easily.'

This seemed to Saoirse even more ridiculous than her

'three spirits' statement.

'Better for *you*, maybe!' she said and tried out a couple of the staccato punches to the belly that her grandfather had taught her.

'I never met anybody who was so tough that they could take a couple of shots to the breadbasket and keep smiling,' Francis Tory had told her, but obviously he had never met Spin Zhuk, because Spin not only took the shots but seemed to absorb them without any adverse effects.

'Over the side and no more complaining,' said Spin, as though trying to persuade a stubborn child to take her medicine. 'I have many works to do.'

Saoirse attempted to wriggle free, but Spin Zhuk had restrained much bigger people as recently as the previous Tuesday, when she'd had a run-in with a Russian kettlebell champion who had objected to Spin stealing his Humvee. So to the Ukrainian wheelwoman, a fifteen-year-old slip of an Irish girl provided little in the way of a challenge. Spin flipped Saoirse upside down, pinning her arms behind her back and pinioning Saoirse's legs with her chin, of all things.

Unfortunately, she neglected to secure Saoirse's second-deadliest weapon, her mouth, which had a direct line to her ultimate weapon, her brain.

Saoirse realized that Spin was agitated because Saoirse was supposed to be dead. Spin had sworn to her beloved *chef* that she had done the evil deed. If it turned out that Saoirse was alive, which it had and she was, then there would be trouble in the camp.

So Saoirse yelled, 'I am alive! Saoirse Tory is alive!'

Spin immediately realized her mistake and blocked Saoirse's mouth with the handiest stopper, which happened to be her own fist – a fist that had little stifling effect on the Iron Man helmet. And this was how the Mandarin found them both when he strode onto the bridge.

It was such a bizarre tableau that the Mandarin could not help laughing.

'This is curious,' he said, wiping an imaginary tear. 'Two living girls where there should be one. What I would like, Miss Zhuk, is for you to kindly explain to me, without frills or evasions, exactly what is happening here.'

'Yes, chef,' said Spin, obviously nervous. 'There were some circumstances –'

This was as far as she got before the Mandarin lunged with extraordinary speed across the bridge, forcing the Zhuk/Tory combo against the bulkhead. But that was not the worst of it. The worst was that four of the Mandarin's dreaded rings were now jabbed painfully into Spin's left cheekbone.

'Choose,' he said to Spin Zhuk.

'Please, chef,' said Spin, trying to turn her face away, but she was pinned to the jolly photo of a fisherman drinking a beer, a photo that had always seemed out of place on this vessel built purely for war.

'Miss Zhuk, you have lied to me and, even worse, failed me. Choose a ring and let fate decide whether you live or die.'

Spin's eyeballs swivelled as she tried to somehow see the rings pressed into her cheekbone. It was impossible, and she could not escape the chef's grip. He was a master of many martial arts. Spin had once witnessed him disable an entire special forces unit without spilling the cup of jasmine tea he was drinking. Granted, the cup had a lid, but it was still an impressive feat. Spin had seen all ten rings in operation that day and knew that many of them had a fatal sting.

One unleashed an ice blast.

Another was a mento-intensifier, allowing mind control.

There was a flame blaster.

A white light electromagnetic energy manipulator.

An electric-shock emitter.

And others she could not remember now.

'Which finger, Spin?' asked the Mandarin. 'Or should I choose for you, perhaps?'

'Index,' blurted Spin, and there was a tinge of animal desperation in her normally even tone. 'Index, chef.'

'I just want you to know,' said the Mandarin softly, 'that whatever happens now, our slate is clean.'

Spin Zhuk took what was possibly her last breath and held it. The Mandarin put his thumb on the scanner at the back of his index-finger ring, sending two tiny spikes into Spin Zhuk's cheek. Spin felt them and knew what was coming.

'Oh –' she said, and probably intended to follow that up with some choice swear words, but the surge of five thousand volts through the Mandarin's ring put all thought of speech out of her mind. Every muscle in Spin Zhuk's body tensed so violently that she cracked her jaw and two teeth before passing out on the deck. The Mandarin was insulated from the shock by his ring and stepped back quickly so as not to be in the current circuit, but Saoirse got enough of a shock to propel her across the bridge as though she had been swatted by a giant.

Leveque had just stepped onto the bridge in time to see the punishment being carried out.

'Mon dieu,' he said. 'Ze electro blast. I 'ate zat one. It leaves ze mark.'

The Mandarin shook his hand to cool down the ring, which always overheated a little.

'Freddie, I do think you are actually trying to provoke me. Be a good fellow and make sure Miss Zhuk has not swallowed her tongue while I feed our stowaway to the fish.'

Leveque was disappointed that he would not be allowed to jettison the extra cargo, but he had the good sense to keep it to himself.

'*Oui*, chef. *Immédiatement*.' He felt it safer to stick to his native tongue in case another mispronunciation slipped out.

The Mandarin crossed the bridge and was about to grab Saoirse's leg to drag her out when he heard a voice that was not Saoirse's coming from the region of her head.

The helmet was receiving a transmission.

'Hang on, kid,' said the voice, leaking out through the now fully charged helmet's neck hole. 'I'm coming to get you. Stay hidden and stay safe.'

Far from being irritated by Tony Stark's insistence on continuing to breathe and insert himself in the operation, the Mandarin was actually pleased that he would have another crack at the billionaire. He had hated to see his prey escape – though he was not yet certain how it had happened – for it was his habit to crush the very soul of his adversaries in the moments before he destroyed their bodies. He'd had a very particular soul-crushing message for Tony Stark. The thought that he might yet deliver this message lifted his spirits considerably – so much so that he was glad Spin would survive the rings.

The Mandarin squatted beside Saoirse and waited for Stark's next message, which came a few seconds later.

'Use your brain, kid,' said the faint voice. 'Stay low and keep that big mouth shut.'

The Mandarin smiled again. The child *was* staying low, no doubt about that.

'And yes, Stark,' he said aloud, though the billionaire could not hear him, 'she does have a big mouth, but it will be staying shut for quite a while. Perhaps forever.'

It occurred to the Mandarin then that in American movies this would be precisely the moment when the bad guy indulged in a maniacal laugh. Because the idea amused him, he allowed himself a brief guffaw.

'Ha-ha-haaaa!' he cried, shaking his fist for good measure.

The creepiest thing about the moment was not the laugh itself but the way the Mandarin cut it off like a tap when he grew bored with the notion.

'Come, Tony Stark,' he said to the helmet. 'Come and hear what it is I must tell you before I end your life. Perhaps the hearing alone will be enough to stop your heart.'

Saoirse had awoken just in time to catch the movie-villain laugh, and she knew that had it been an actual movie, she would have turned it off immediately. But this was no movie; it was life. And sometimes the truth was stranger than fiction. This was one of those times.

A NEAPOLITAN FLATBREAD

The *Tanngrisnir*

Diavolo Conroy was often asked whether he had Italian ancestors, given his unusual first name. He would lie and say that he had been named for the brigand in the novels of his mother's favourite author, Alexandre Dumas. Diavolo lied because the truth was too embarrassing to relate. The *truth* was that Diavolo Conroy's mother had met her husband-to-be over a pizza in Rome and as a tribute to her new favourite meal had chosen the Italian name for her firstborn. The irony was, as his father later told him, that the meal had been a flatbread, not a pizza at all, and for double irony points, his father also confided that the flatbread in question had not actually been a

Diavolo but a Neapolitan. So it was not a story Diavolo got into if he could help it, as it was impossible to come out of it with his dignity intact.

I suppose it could have been worse, he often thought. *If Mammy had eaten pastry that day, I might have been named Croissant Conroy.*

He decided now, behind the wheel of the *Tanngrisnir*, that if he survived the day he would share the story with the Stark fella, because he'd been dying to tell someone for years and Tony Stark seemed like he would enjoy a good irony-heavy tale.

In truth, Diavolo was only ruminating on this old story in the first place because he was trying not to think about the ordeal that surely lay ahead.

'Oh my god,' he said aloud. 'My life is flashing before me.'

And everyone knew what that meant.

'Now, now, Diavolo boy,' he told himself. 'Don't be getting the trousers in a twist. It's perfectly natural to muse on formative events before an engagement.'

That was something he'd picked up during a psychology of conflict lecture when he'd been doing his master's at UCD.

In fact, that wasn't the full sentence in that lecture. He usually tried not to recall the full sentence, because it was too painful, but he could think about it now that it might be his last chance. The full sentence was: 'It's perfectly natural to muse on formative events *and lifelong regrets* before an engagement.'

Regrets – he had a few.

The main one being that he and his wife Siobhan (pronounced Shive-*awn*) had never had a child of their own. They had tried everything, and nothing did the trick. Diavolo adored his wife and his life, and they both believed that a child would make things just about perfect.

If I make it through this, thought Inspector Conroy, *I'm going to sit down with my darling Shiv and discuss adoption.*

Had Tony Stark been there, he would doubtless have pointed out that Diavolo's pet name for his wife was also American prison slang for a concealed blade. So it was just as well that Stark was off rescuing Saoirse. The last thing Diavolo Conroy needed in his life right at this moment was another joke about Conroy first names.

'Focus on the mission, Diavolo boy,' Inspector Conroy told himself. There would be time enough to think about adoption later.

He hoped.

The mission was this: full steam ahead to the Royal G to lend whatever support he could to the ground forces protecting the environmental ministers. Stark had been against the plan, arguing that there were more than enough troops at the Royal G to deal with the Mandarin's people, which would not number more than two, but Inspector Conroy had insisted. The ministers were his responsibility and he had already left his post once, as it were. His duty was on that beach, where the Mandarin's attack would surely focus.

'The Mandarin won't be there himself,' Stark had assured Conroy. 'That's not his MO. Our sneaky Mandarin pal likes to put distance between himself and the actual op zone, in case things go wrong. In all the attacks he's been associated with, there has never been a scrap of physical evidence that he was in the area. Maybe that's why he's eluded the authorities for so long.'

So Stark was following Saoirse Tory's signal, which had split off from the boat's projected course, and Conroy was on the boat's tail, having phoned in the threat.

The Mandarin's buckos will have quite the surprise waiting for them, thought Diavolo Conroy, fervently hoping that he would be in time for the party.

Though perhaps party *is the wrong term,* he thought. *"Flaming gun battle" may be closer to the mark.*

Whichever it was to be, Inspector Conroy was determined that his men on shore would not face the challenge alone.

Tony Stark had made many mistakes in his life, including the time when, as a toddler, he had swallowed a sea anemone and been subjected to a robust stomach pumping. And then there was the time when, as an adult, he had taken Rhodey's beloved Harley for a spin straight into a post and been subjected to a robust stomach thumping. There was also the time he had mistakenly turned up in costume for the president's dinner at the White House. He had for some reason thought that the idea was to dress *as* a president, and he'd chosen to attend as Abraham Bling-con, which was a gold lamé version of the original. It was a major media faux pas that had insulted the entire nation in one swoop and gotten more than half a billion hits on YouTube.

But the mistake he had made on this day was far worse, because it could cost lives. This particular mistake was one of judgment, in that Tony had underestimated the Mandarin's determination to see the job done. This mistake was compounded by his assumption that the Mandarin's boat was a run-of-the-mill high-tech gunship, when in reality it was beyond anything even Howard Stark could have dreamed of. In fact, the boat had almost as much destructive power at its disposal as a low-yield nuclear weapon.

The Mandarin had named his boat the *Ajax*, after the man who had supervised the construction of the Trojan horse. He thought the name apt, because much like the famed wooden horse, his gunship was a wolf in sheep's clothing. On the outside it resembled a deep-sea fishing trawler, but underneath the double hull lurked a sleek war machine carrying next-generation kill tech.

In truth, committing the *Ajax* to combat had not been the Mandarin's original plan. He would have preferred to have Iron Man take both credit and blame, keeping the *Ajax* in reserve until the next mission, but even the greatest plans sometimes needed to adapt as the operation progressed.

As Spin Zhuk piloted the gunboat up the narrow inlet leading to the Royal G's yacht dock, it seemed clumsy and out of place nuzzling through the luxury craft – but not half as out of place as it was about to seem.

On the bridge, Spin Zhuk and Freddie Leveque had changed into their combat gear and were clothed from head to toe in battle armour. Their backs and legs bristled with barrels and blades, and their features were obscured by glare-resistant faceplates.

Spin was using a joystick to nudge the *Ajax* closer to the jetty, forcing a path through the luxury craft. The dock, not fifty feet away, was lined with black-suited secret service and national security guys, all gesticulating or talking into the palms of their hands.

'Look at zese idiots,' said Freddie. 'With zere black suits and wrist radios. Zey are like ze catwalk models sniffing perfume.'

Zhuk urged the *Ajax* to within twenty feet of the jetty. 'Come on, Freddie. Be paying attention now. I am not wishing to face the chef's rings another time.'

Leveque saluted. 'I hear you, partner.'

'Are you ready to be rocking?'

Leveque wiggled his fingers over the weapons control bank like a pianist about to attempt Rachmaninoff's "Piano Concerto No. 3". 'Ready,' he said.

The radio blared with warnings from the shore, with

the various security forces shouting over each other, all saying things along the lines of, 'Come out on deck' and 'Prepare to be boarded, or we will open fire.'

Leveque switched off the radio. 'Blah, blah, blah,' he said. 'Zese guys have no idea. Zey should shoot zere weapons and not zere mouths. Are we in range of ze main building?'

'We are in range,' confirmed Spin.

'Zen it is time for the wolf to shed ze clothing of ze sheep.'

'Did you say *ship* or *sheep*?' Spin asked.

'Both,' said Freddie, and he brought his palm down on a red button that he privately called the Transformer.

Two of the black-suited men standing on the shoreline were on Inspector Diavolo Conroy's team, and one was in contact with the boss by phone.

'It's just a fishing boat,' said the man, whose name was Fergal. 'I'm telling you, Dave, some dimwit net hauler is trying to land on the wrong jetty. You'd think all the yachts would tip him off, wouldn't you?'

Conroy's voice came back crackly over the speaker. 'First, don't call me Dave, Fergal, or I will reach through this phone and yank out your voice box. And second, am I not just this minute telling you that the hostiles have probably disguised their craft to get through global waters?'

'Yeah, that's right, Dave ... sir,' said Fergal rolling his

eyes. 'It's a transformer trawler.'

Fergal winked at his partner and mouthed, *Watch this*. His partner groaned, because Fergal was well-known for messing with old Spicy Pizza Diavolo, and this did not seem like the time.

'Hold on, sir,' said Fergal. 'There's something happening here.'

'What's happening?' asked Conroy. 'What do you see?'

'I don't believe it,' said Fergal. 'The fishing boat, it's sprouted wings. There are tentacles coming out of the portholes.'

Conroy bought it for a second, then: 'Fergal, there are lives at stake here. You better pray for a reassignment on another planet, because when I catch up with you there will be hell to pay and I'm presenting the bill.'

Fergal laughed into his fist, but his laughter stuck like a lump of coal in his throat when he saw what was really happening to the fishing boat.

'Okay, sir. Now I'm going to hold up my phone and show you what's actually going on.'

'Why don't you just tell me?' asked Conroy.

'Because you would never believe it, especially after the wings and tentacles.'

Fergal held up the phone, and even though Diavolo could see the fishing boat transforming before his eyes, he still had trouble believing what was going on.

'I'll be there in two minutes,' he said tersely. 'Hold them off until then.'

The fishing boat continued to shed its skin, and Fergal thought:

Two minutes. He'll never make it in time.

THE TIGER AND THE ROAR

The assembled security forces had been feeling pretty smug about getting out in front of the terrorist threat. Environmental ministers were not exactly high-priority targets, so the Royal G had not been chosen for its easily defendable position or bombproof bunker but because it had a world-class spa and a golf course where both Tiger Woods and Rory McIlroy had teed off.

As the saying goes in the golf world, *If it's good enough for the Tiger and the Roar ...*

Even so, each minister or representative travelled with a bunch of his or her own secret service agents, most of whom were ex-special forces, plus there was a platoon of actual special forces soldiers stationed in the estate mews just in case. As it happened, just in case had just come to pass. This meant a total of fifty-odd troops all packing at least two weapons each but zero heavy ordnance, which put them at a disadvantage. However, all was not lost, because Ireland is a small country and the big guns were already on the way from the nearest army base. In addition, two Westland troop rapid-response choppers had been scrambled and would arrive in minutes.

Unfortunately for the various environmental ministers and their aides, protectors and caterers, none of these security measures would make a bit of difference, because the *Ajax* was like nothing ever seen before on Earth. If the soldiers were honest, at least half of them seriously considered running far away as soon as the craft revealed itself.

The scene that unfolded on the North Dublin seafront went a little like this:

Freddie Leveque pressed the button and several things happened to the innocuous-looking trawler. First, over two hundred explosive bolts detonated simultaneously, or as near to it as makes no difference, sending two dozen planks of false hull sliding into the ocean. Where there had been pitted and scarred wood, there was now reinforced armoured plating dotted with weapons ports. Which brings us nicely to the second thing that happened: automatic cannons of various calibres whirred from their stowage beds, slotting through the weapons ports until the *Ajax* resembled a giant, potentially very violent metal hedgehog. Third, there was a mortar *whoomp* as the ship shot a low-altitude tethered surveillance satellite into the lower atmosphere to give Freddie Leveque and Spin Zhuk a bird's eye view of the combat zone. Though, as Leveque had noted, 'It's not really a combat zone, you know. It is a demolition zone.'

The aft cabin suddenly went mobile; it was shunted ten feet up to the top of the central mast by a pneumatic vertical track system, which allowed Freddie Leveque a 360-degree field of fire with his fifty-cal repeater and various launchers and harpoons. The watchers onshore were then disoriented by blinding light that was beamed down from solar cameras on the satellite receiver and flashed from banks of projectors on the gunwales.

All this was impressive but not insurmountable for the security forces, who reacted as they had been trained to react: by opening fire. They sent a stream of lead flying in the general direction of the wailing wall of white light, inside of which lay the *Ajax*. Only twenty percent of the shots hit the craft, and every slug that struck home bounced off with no more effect than a penny bouncing off a wall.

High up in his gun tower, Leveque was in complete control of the weaponry.

'We are destroying zese idiots,' he said gleefully into his mouthpiece. 'Zey 'ave no clue what is 'appening.'

'Hit the main building,' said Spin from below on the bridge. 'Then we pull out.'

Leveque strafed the shoreline with machine-gun fire

from twin mini-guns.

'Zere is no 'urry,' he said. 'Ze chef said to do a full test.'

'Fire the SPIKE, Leveque,' said Zhuk. 'We have choppers incoming.'

Leveque rolled his eyes. '*Eh bien*. I am firing ze SPIKE.'

Freddie Leveque used a joystick to aim a harpoon-like missile, though strictly speaking it had a five-kilometre footprint and didn't really need aiming, as long as it activated more than fifty metres away from the *Ajax*'s shields.

'*Bonne chance*, Monsieur SPIKE,' said Leveque, and he fired the missile. It sped in a tight spiral towards the main hotel building, which lay a hundred metres back from the coast. The SPIKE tore a chunk out of an old-timey bell tower and then *thunked* into the main lobby.

'Ze eye of ze bull,' said Leveque, and then he tapped the flare guard on his visor up a few notches. Looking directly into the glow of the SPIKE could damage a person's eyes. On the bridge below, Spin Zhuk keyed up her own flare guard and patted herself down to check that all her weapons were present and correct. Zhuk favoured blanket bombing, but the chef insisted that was too clumsy, and people often survived an earthquake's dumping an entire building on their heads, so they needed helmet cam confirmation for each of the five targets.

Once the SPIKE activated, Leveque and Spin Zhuk would venture onshore, pick their way through the wailing wounded and track down the ministers. And anyone who could have stopped them would be in no condition to do anything.

The SPIKE didn't look like much when it activated. The armoured plates dropped from the nose cone to reveal three triangular plates of reflective cells. There was a blaze of light like an old-fashioned magnesium flare, and then the whole thing melted into a pile of running slop. Any kid watching the process would have given the experience a two on the *meh* scale – before their eyes started to burn. In fact, two members of the German security detail were much relieved to see that the giant harpoon-looking gizmo that had thudded through the wall seemed to have malfunctioned. But what went on outside the visible spectrum was much more impressive. Then the SPIKE did what it was ingeniously designed to do, which was as follows:

(1) It piggybacked on the nearest network within range to emit a sonic Taser blast, which rendered anyone hooked up to an earpiece practically immobile for fifteen minutes. I say 'practically immobile' because, for some reason even the designers were not able to understand, the victims' organs and eyeballs kept functioning. So there was lots of rolling eyes and shallow breathing but not much else.

(2) Once the sonic Taser had been broadcast, taking every member of all the security forces out of the game, the SPIKE emitted a localized electromagnetic pulse that

knocked out every battery or mains-powered gadget, vehicle, or comm system in its five-kilometre footprint.

Essentially: game over. Except on the *Ajax*, where the systems were magnetically protected.

Up in his aerie, Freddie Leveque clapped delightedly as a chopper fell from the sky two kilometres to the north.

'Ze SPIKE,' he said. 'I love zis acronym. What are ze letters again?'

Spin Zhuk was out on deck, extending a bridge to shore. 'It is so stupid. One of the chef's jokes.'

'Are you saying ze chef is stupid? Is zat what you are saying?'

Spin guided the extension bridge with a phone app. 'No, I am not saying this. I would never say this.'

'Well, zen tell me the letters.'

'Very well. S-P-I-K-E. Sonic Pulse Interference Kaboom-E.'

Leveque chuckled. '*Kaboomee.* Zat is my favourite part.'

It was typical of Leveque that he could laugh and joke while spread before them were death and pain. Spin could see plumes of smoke rising from six crash sites at least, and dozens of security operatives lay on the ground, frozen like statues by the sonic Taser. She was thankful that Cole Vanger was no longer with the group, or he would have torched these people for fun. Spin knew that she was far from being an angel, and she would kill them, too, but only if she was being paid to do it.

'Let's go, Leveque. The Taser lasts fifteen to thirty minutes only.'

'So what?' said Freddie, unperturbed. 'After zat, we shoot zem. No problem.'

But there was a problem coming their way. And he was coming at high speed, with zero control over his approach.

Inspector Diavolo Conroy had taken full advantage of the *Tanngrisnir*'s revolutionary 3-D printer to make a range of weapons, and he coded each gun and rocket launcher to his own thumbprint.

At least I'll die well armed, he had thought.

But he didn't really fancy dying that day and leaving Shiv on her own.

I will just have to emerge victorious so.

The men on the shore were top-string fellas, Conroy knew. But he also remembered what Stark had told him: 'You're going up against world-class operatives, so be careful. Just contain them until old Starkey here shows up. No offence, Diavolo – I still can't believe your parents did that to you, by the way – no offence, D, but this is a fight for Super Heroes.'

This kind of talk would make any Irishman on the planet switch into uber-sarcastic mode, and Conroy was no exception.

'That's right, T, you're a Super Hero. Sure I don't know what we did at all, *at all*, before you got here. It's a wonder the entire island didn't sink into the sea out of sheer helplessness.'

Stark had laughed. 'You tickle me, Conroy. But seriously, watch your back, and one more thing.'

'What thing would that me, Mr Super Hero?'

'Don't put a scratch on my yacht.'

As it happened, Conroy was raised in a boatyard, and when he hadn't been playing the Irish national sport of hurling, he had been tinkering with rich people's yachts and sailing them down to Monaco or Cannes or the like; so the basic controls of the *Tanngrisnir* quickly yielded to his expert touch. As soon as Iron Man's repulsor glare had faded, Conroy had opened the throttle, lifting the *Tanngrisnir* onto its metal fins and retracting the stubby mast.

He had a feeling that time was of the essence, a feeling that was confirmed by Fergal's call.

A few seconds could be the difference between life and death, Conroy knew.

The Mandarin's boat was actually in view now, and Conroy watched in amazement as it transformed from a fishing trawler into a gunship.

'Ah, here now,' he said. 'What's the story here?'

'The story?' said Prototony's secondary module over the bridge's speakers. The AI was a stripped-down version that didn't have much of the original's sparkle. 'This is not a story, Inspector Conroy. This is reality. That fishing vessel has revealed itself to be in fact a gunship.'

'I was hoping for a bit more detail. Are we at

full speed?'

'Are you referring to the speed of light? That would be full speed.'

'I mean top speed for this boat. Can you open it up a little?'

'That's all she's got,' said Prototony. 'Which is a lot more than what we're about to have if I'm right about that missile the gunship has just fired.'

Conroy felt his stomach sink. 'What about that missile?'

'Two words,' said Prototony Lite. 'Electromagnetic pulse.'

'Isn't that three words?' asked Diavolo, but Prototony had already shut itself down to preserve whatever it could of the system before the EMP hit, leaving Inspector Conroy behind the wheel of a fifty-ton lump of aquaplaning metal.

EMP, thought Conroy. *Meaning that the wheel I am behind will momentarily become useless and this speeding boat will go wherever it's pointed.*

Having realized this, Inspector Conroy pointed the *Tanngrisnir* where he wanted it to go.

And just in time, because no sooner had he yanked the wheel than every electrical system on the yacht died and Diavolo felt about as in control as a barnacle on a whale's back.

Luckily, the captain's chair seat belt had no electrical components, so Conroy was able to strap in before impact – at which point the grid above the captain's chair, which Conroy had not noticed, dropped twenty-five gallons of compression gel that congealed around his frame, turning him into what looked like an enormous blob of mucous and saving him from certain death.

It was quite possible that Leveque's change of expression ranked among the fastest ever achieved. One millisecond he was smug and bloodthirsty; the next he was comically amazed, not to mention flying through the air in the wreckage of his crow's nest. The amazed expression changed pretty quickly, too, into slack-jawed unconsciousness, as he was knocked out by a concussive charge that did not explode but rather clocked him on the temple with its timing mechanism. So to recap: he was clocked into concussion by the clock on a concussive charge.

Stark's yacht had rammed the *Ajax* at such a speed that the keel snapped right off its fins and literally boarded the second boat. This assault took the legs out from under Leveque's crow's nest so cleanly that the structure landed on the bridge of Stark's yacht, crashing through the ceiling and smashing the computer banks and control panels.

Conroy remembered Tony's words – 'Don't put a scratch on my yacht' – and thought, *Oops.*

It was a hysterical thought, really, as Conroy's situation was so unbelievable that half of him thought he was lying in a coma somewhere and dreaming the whole adventure.

If my eyes don't deceive me, then I am sitting on the bridge of Iron Man's yacht having double-deckered the Mandarin's gunboat.

There's no way in the name of little green leprechauns that this is actually happening.

But happening or not, he should proceed as though what he was seeing was reality, because if it *was* reality, then surely some terrorist type would be along to skewer him with something sharp any second.

Perhaps you're already skewered, Diavolo boy.

Conroy moved his hand slowly through the compression gel, which stank to high heaven – something he would have to mention to Stark – and unlocked his safety belt. Then he poked a hole in the gel and wiggled himself out. Most of the blob collapsed onto the deck, but a slimy residue clung to Diavolo Conroy, pasting his blond hair flat to his skull.

I feel like I got sneezed out by a giant, he thought, and when he caught sight of himself in an unbroken pane of glass, he realized that he also *looked* like he got sneezed out by a giant.

Conroy checked himself as best he could and was relieved to find that, aside from a painful safety-belt burn across his chest, he seemed remarkably undamaged. That was more than he could say for the boat itself, which was crumpled like a discarded candy wrapper.

Now that Conroy had survived, his survival instincts

kicked in. He searched for his printed weapons, which lay strewn around the deck, only to find that not one was operational.

Of course. The EMP, he realized. He had coded the weapons to his thumbprints, so they had electronic components.

All fried. All I have left is ...

Diavolo had printed two more things.

A hurley and a small hard ball.

For those unfamiliar with the Irish national sport of hurling, it could be fairly described as hockey meets martial arts. Two groups of players armed with wooden sticks, called hurleys, push themselves to the limits of human physicality to put a small leather ball into the other team's goal. On seeing a video reel of the All-Ireland final, famous Japanese writer Yukio Mishima was heard to describe the players as possessing 'the spirits of samurai,' such was their skill with the hurling stick.

Diavolo Conroy could fairly be said to have the spirit of a samurai and had been a rising star in the sport until he blew out his knee coming down from a six-foot midair clash with a two-hundred-pound full back from Galway. Conroy was never happier than when he had a hurley and ball to fool around with, and he'd thought earlier that as long as he had a 3-D printer at his disposal, he might as well print up something to keep his hands busy.

So he had run off the world's first 3-D printed hurley and *sliotar*, as the hard little ball was called. Diavolo found the hurley now underneath a smashed monitor. The ball was nowhere in sight.

Conroy picked up the hurley and felt instantly calmer.

Feels pretty good, he thought. *Even better than the real thing, to quote the U2 lads.*

He'd barely had time to twirl the stick when Freddie Leveque – or as Conroy instantly thought of him, *big burly man who wants to kill me* – came crashing through the ceiling with a wider range of weapons at his disposal than a *Call of Duty* character. Perhaps they were active and perhaps not. Diavolo wasn't about to take any chances.

'Stay where you are, bucko,' said Conroy. 'You are under all sorts of arrest.'

Leveque removed his helmet and shook his head to clear the stars he was seeing, then executed a backflip from a prone position, which Conroy would have thought impossible – but then again, a lot of impossible things were happening that day.

'You would arrest Freddie Leveque wiz a stick?' said the man, and he grinned like a wolf that has spotted a hunk of unguarded bloody meat.

Conroy did not think that particular smile boded well for him.

'It's not just a stick,' he said. 'It's a hurling stick.'

'Well, in zat case …' said Leveque, reaching towards his thigh holster.

Conroy moved pretty fast for a guy with a bum knee, and he rapped Leveque's knuckles with the hurley. 'Don't do it, big boy. I will batter you into the middle of next week.'

Leveque dropped the gun and danced backwards, sucking his knuckles.

'What is zis? We are not in ze schoolyard.'

What would Stark say? Conroy asked himself, then said, 'We're *not* in the schoolyard, pal. We're on my playground now.'

Leveque frowned. 'What is zis meaning? *Playground?* Zis is no playground. You are crazy.'

He reached for a second weapon and Conroy whacked it clear out of his hand with the hurley, sending the pistol skittering across the deck.

No longer wasting time on words, Leveque launched himself through the air, somehow bringing his knees up to bash Conroy in the chest and sending him staggering backwards. As Conroy was staggering, Leveque managed to balance on the inspector's chest, maintaining his own altitude and dishing out several punches to the Irishman's shoulders and face.

As he was being beaten backward, pain sensors flaring white, Conroy realized that the terrorist had some serious combat skills. *I will have to dig deep to get out of this clash alive.*

Leveque, for his part, was outraged that a crazy Irish guy had somehow disabled the most advanced combat craft in the world. But he was grateful that the crazy Irish guy had survived so he could kill him.

Leveque spotted an exposed overhead pipe and

grabbed it. He ran up Conroy's body, finishing the move by smashing the unfortunate inspector in the forehead with both heels. The Irish policeman dropped to his knees and skidded across the deck until he was brought up short by a jumbled pile of electronics.

The barely conscious Conroy thought, *This is it. I can't take this guy. Goodbye, Shiv.*

But even thinking his darling wife's name lit a spark of determination in Conroy's heart.

No. Shiv wants a family, and I will not leave her without one.

Conroy still had his hurley in one hand, but it was of little use at this distance, and his enemy was reaching for a shotgun strapped to his back. Only a fool brought a stick to a shotgun fight.

There must be something, Conroy thought desperately.

And there *was* something, sitting there between his knees.

The *sliotar*. The hurling ball. It was fate.

'Rise up, men of Ireland,' said Conroy, blood dripping from his lips. 'Rise up and be counted.'

'More nonsense, *mon ami*,' said Freddie Leveque. 'I am tired of zis.'

And as the mercenary's fingers found the shotgun's stock, Diavolo Conroy launched into a sequence of moves he had completed so many times in his hurling career that they were named after him.

When a player is fouled in hurling, they receive a free shot. The accepted upper scoring range for the free-shot taker is perhaps a hundred and thirty metres. Young Diavolo Conroy had developed a system of explosive movement from a kneeling position that added impetus to his swing and distance to the shot. His coach had nicknamed this style of free-taking the Diavolo Special, and for a while it had been quite popular on the youth circuit. This was the action Conroy's body opted for now, when faced with the most dangerous enemy of his career.

Leveque had eight shells in his pump-action shotgun.

Diavolo Conroy had one ball. One chance.

Leveque talked as he moved, which was a bad habit of his that the Mandarin had warned him would get him in trouble one day.

'*Mon dieu, c'est terrible*. What a day. First zis Iron Man guy, and now zis little leprechaun policeman. Enough. *C'est fini*.'

As he spoke, he yanked the shotgun from its magnetic holder on his back and pumped a round into the chamber. At this range the load would take the Irishman's head clean off his shoulders, and perhaps then Freddie would feel a little better.

I can still eliminate ze ministers, he realized. *Zere is time.*

Leveque aimed the barrel at his enemy, who seemed to be making some kind of attempt to save himself.

But what matter? Escape is impossible.

Not impossible, as it turned out, but very difficult.

From a kneeling position, Diavolo Conroy led with his chest, lurching forwards in a movement that seemed almost apelike. He dipped his head, dropping his centre of gravity, and whipped his hurl arm back until the tendons screamed.

You're getting old, Diavolo, he told himself. *Old and stiff.*

With his right hand he scooped up the hard ball, slotting the ridges between his fingers, and then, pistoning his legs, he literally catapulted forwards towards Leveque just as the man's finger closed around the shotgun trigger.

Time seemed to slow as Conroy threw the ball in the air, then whipped the hurl around to connect. It was a solid strike, and the ball sped straight and true, directly into Leveque's eye socket. The Frenchman reared back as he pulled the trigger, causing his shotgun blast to pull high and over Conroy's head.

Leveque was out cold before he hit the deck. He was actually lucky not to be dead, as Conroy's strike had put pressure on his eyeball, forcing it into his skull. Two more millimetres and his brain would have exploded. Freddie Leveque was out of the game, and Inspector Conroy had beaten the odds and survived.

Conroy's Diavolo Special took him across the destroyed deck, where he actually landed on top of Leveque.

'This is awkward,' he said to the unconscious Frenchman, then gingerly plucked the hurling ball from the man's eye socket and grimaced when he saw the mashed orb below, which seemed to be leaking some kind of fluid.

Conroy rolled off Leveque and onto his own back.

He thought about how much he wanted to see his wife and then about how teed-off Stark would be when he saw his boat.

'Sure that fella is always going on how he's a billionaire,' he muttered. 'He can build himself another one.'

SOMETHING FISHY

London, England, one hour later

It felt good being back in the red-and-gold rig, skimming over wave tops at high speed. Usually, Tony liked to break in new battle suits with a rigorous test flight, but there was no time for that now. The girl Saoirse was in danger, and in spite of the circumstances of their recent meeting, Tony could not help admiring the lengths she had gone to trying to rescue her sister.

Spiking my AI, he thought. *That was pretty darn clever.*

So he would follow the signal from the Party Pack's helmet and rescue the Irish girl while Inspector Conroy went directly toward the Royal G, where the signal had been headed before it swerved off.

'I have no choice, Tony boy,' the man called Diavolo

(of all things) had told him back on the *Tanngrisnir*. 'The Royal G is where most of the ministers are holed up. It can't be a coincidence. My duty is there.'

Tony had told him to call ahead and have the troops ready and he himself would follow on to the Royal G just as soon as he cleared up the Mandarin mess.

The Mandarin won't be at the attack site. He never is.

No, it was more than likely that the Mandarin would be with the hostage if he had discovered Saoirse.

Prototony cut in on his thoughts. 'Hey, T-Star, we have an incoming call from the helmet. You wanna take it?'

Saoirse, you smart kid, thought Tony. *You got out.*

'Of course I want to take it,' he said. 'Put it up.'

'Could you say, "Put it up, P-Tone"? That would mean a lot.'

Tony scowled. If this AI's personality was learned from his own public behaviour, then he could see why people thought he was irritating. And he knew people found him irritating, because Rhodey had told him so. His actual words were: 'Tony, man, you are the most reviled person on the Internet. There are a couple of teenybopper bad boys who come close, but you, my man, are numero uno. You're too showy. You know what you do, man? You flaunt. You're a flaunter.'

And then, because they'd been pitching a couple of balls at the time, Tony had chased Rhodey with a bat and somehow the wing mirror on Rhodey's Trans Am had gotten smashed, and they hadn't spoken for a week afterward.

Tony didn't have time to argue with Prototony; he barely had time to *think* about arguing with Prototony.

'Okay, okay,' he said. 'Could you please put the call up, P-Tone?'

'You got it, T-Star.'

The heads-up display on the faceplate's inner surface crackled, and a distorted face appeared.

'Saoirse!' said Tony. 'Thank goodness. What kind of crazy moves did you pull to escape that maniac?'

But when the static settled, Tony saw that the face on the display was not Saoirse's but the Mandarin's.

'Mandarin, if you've hurt her, I swear I'll –' said Tony.

'Ah,' said the Mandarin, 'the implied threat. How trite. How cliché. How uniquely *American*, if you don't mind me saying. A bankrupt vocabulary to go along with your bankrupt ideology. The land of the free? Not according to the health insurance figures.'

Tony clenched his jaw so tightly it cracked, and he spoke through gritted teeth. 'Is that why you called me, Mandy? To give me a lecture on the evils of Western civilization?'

'No,' admitted the Mandarin. 'That was off topic, as you might say. No, Mr Stark. I called you to deliver a message.'

'Don't tell me – stay away or the kid dies, right?'

'No. Oh, no. Most certainly not. Come and find me, Mr Stark. You shall not escape twice.'

'So, what, you're just calling to say hi?'

The Mandarin smiled. 'Yes, of course. Hi! But also, come *alone* or the child dies. You see, that is how to make a threat. State the consequences clearly.'

'I'm coming, Mandarin. And let me clear up any fogginess regarding my implied threat. Whatever injury you have visited upon that girl, I shall visit the same injury upon you. Is that plain enough?'

The Mandarin nodded as if considering that. 'It is quite clever actually, as it forces me to examine my own actions. Well done, Stark. But though I relish our meeting, I feel we are unfairly matched. After all, you have your wonderful suit.'

'You've got those mystical rings of yours.'

'This is true. My rings are indeed powerful. But still, I think in the interests of fair play, I need to tilt the scales a little in my favour.'

Tony knew he should shut down the call right away and follow the signal to its source – after all, his systems put his ETA at four minutes – but the curious side of him kept the line open.

'"Tilt the scales" ... And how are you gonna do that?'

'Like Genghis Khan, who was my direct ancestor, I shall use what we now call psychological warfare. The great Khan employed expert rumour-mongers to spread exaggerations concerning the number of ferocious Mongol horsemen in his army. Often his battles were won before his forces arrived on the battlefield.'

'So, you're gonna make up some lame story to throw me off my game? Seems a little counterproductive to give me the heads-up.'

'There is no need for fabrications, Mr Stark. I have some old news for you that should prove sufficiently disturbing to put you off your game at the very least. In fact, I imagine you will lose all perspective and come blazing in here without caution.'

Prototony broke in on the conversation. 'T-Star, I totally recommend cutting this bozo off. Nothing good can come from hearing him out. He's playing you.'

Tony knew the AI was right, but he was hooked.

'Back off, Prototony. I need to hear this. What's this old news, Mandy? Maybe I'm not as easily spooked as you think.'

'I give you fair warning, Mr Stark. If you choose to hear this news, your life will be forever changed – what little of your life is left. So I offer you one chance to preserve your blissful ignorance.'

'Just spit it out, Mandy.'

'Very well. This story concerns your old colleague Anna Wei. Or perhaps you were more than colleagues, eh, Tony Stark? The famous ladies' man.'

Tony felt suddenly sick in the pit of his stomach, but he could not sever the connection. For years he had been haunted by Anna's death, convinced that she had not in fact killed herself, and now it seemed as though the Mandarin was about to shed some light on the night she plunged into the Pacific.

'Keep talking, Mandarin, but know that this could be the last story you ever tell.'

'Vague threats once again,' said the Mandarin. 'How utterly tedious.'

'You got something to say about Anna, Mandarin? Let's have it.'

'In my memoirs I plan to spend some considerable time on this incident, for I believe it was significant to us both – formative, if you like. But for now, the abbreviated version.'

The only word Tony could think of to describe the Mandarin's expression at that moment was *smug*. Rhodey had a name for a face like that; he called it 'punchably smug,' which Tony had never really gotten until now, probably because he was a pretty smug guy himself most of the time.

'You have long suspected that Anna Wei's life did not end by her own hand, and you were correct in this.'

Tony got such a shock he almost lost control of the suit.

'It was *you*? You killed Anna?'

The Mandarin's smug mask cracked a little in annoyance. 'Please, Stark. I am speaking here. Relating. You are interrupting the flow. There is better to come – or perhaps worse.'

Nothing from Tony. No snappy one-liner. That Stark was gone, and in his place was a coldhearted warrior.

'This was no simple assassination. Preparation is everything,' said the Mandarin. 'My illustrious countryman Sun Tzu said in *The Art of War* that "he will win who, prepared himself, waits to take the enemy unprepared." And so I prepared with great zeal and patience for this important assignment. I employed my spies and laid my plans.'

'I thought this was the abbreviated version,' said Tony, his own voice sounding strange to him.

'Ah, yes. Your arrival is imminent, so I should get to the point. Anna Wei was intensely loyal to you and to her adopted country, so it took all my ingenuity to trick her into working for me. I had a laboratory constructed in an underground compound and staffed exclusively with Americans. Miss Wei was removed from her apartment by what she believed to be S.H.I.E.L.D. operatives and continued her work on psionic control, not knowing that all the time she was perfecting my ring technology.'

Poor, dear Anna, thought Tony. *Kidnapped and tricked.*

'When Miss Wei's work was complete, I tried to manipulate her into hacking the Iron Man suit, but she would not. Regrettably, she was of no further use to me then.'

It was true, Tony knew. Everything made sense. He suddenly felt so angry that in legal terms his mental state at that precise moment would have qualified as temporary insanity.

And still the Mandarin kept talking. 'So Miss Wei is in fact dead, but she did not die by her own hand as the evidence pointed to. For I planted that evidence.'

Tony's heartbeat accelerated into dangerous territory and he could barely control himself enough to compose one short sentence.

'I am coming, Mandarin.'

The Mandarin chortled delightedly. 'Oh, excellent delivery, Tony Stark. It would seem that my plan is already working.'

Tony knew it was true, but he was past caring. The Mandarin had murdered Anna, and in the next few minutes, vengeance would descend from the skies.

The Party Pack helmet put the Mandarin's position somewhere inside a dead zone on a deserted stretch of the Thames's shore outside London, England, four hundred miles southeast of Dublin.

'Great,' said Prototony. 'More docklands. We should find a bridge to melt. Whaddya say, T-Star?'

'Where is he?' asked Tony coldly. 'Exactly.'

'No can do *exactly*. I'm only getting white noise. He must've set up one of his famous signal jammers there. My guess is that it's a megablocker. That area has less signal than the Middle Ages.'

'Where's the dead zone?'

'An abandoned structure on the wharf. Possibly a fish-processing plant. BTW, I love that word, *wharf.* I don't get to use it often.'

'So he's in the plant?'

'The *helmet* is in the plant.'

'That helmet belongs to Stark Industries,' said Tony, and he accelerated toward the building.

The fish factory had been abandoned for so long that it had adopted the muddy colour of its surroundings, as though the Thames's murk had leeched into the building's concrete. In a way it was perfectly camouflaged; from the air it was almost invisible, and casual observers from a passing aircraft would have seen nothing but another stretch of shore. The riverbank itself had been eroded by toxic discharge, and Tony's atmospherix told him that the water was not fit for consumption or even bathing. Needless to say, there was little in the way of marine life. In fact, the only residents in this backwater stretch of the Thames were discarded shopping carts, bicycles and a cluster of laptops, yawning open in the shallows like hungry alligators.

Of human life there was no sign on this side of the river, but the opposite bank was loaded with traffic and office buildings.

'I'm going in,' said Tony.

'I thought you might, T-Star,' said Prototony. 'I'm guessing we won't be doing the penguin?'

'No. Full speed, nose first. Heat up the weapons.'

'I'm nearly afraid to ask, but which ones?'

'All of them,' said Tony.

*

The line between hero and villain is a fine one, and Tony had always managed to stay on the right side of it. Sure, he had made a few tough calls but always for the right reason. Now, with hatred for the Mandarin wrapped around his heart and mind like a parasite, that line seemed faint and unimportant. What was a man if he could not avenge his loved ones? What was morality in the face of real justice? Tony had seen enough to know that the only real justice was the kind you took for yourself. And at that moment he had no real plan beyond saving the girl and making the Mandarin suffer. How far that suffering would go, he could not say.

Tony was two seconds from blowing out the roof panels when he was distracted by the sudden arrival of machine-gun fire, which *rat-a-tatted* against his titanium-alloy armour, jerking his head to the right with the force of impact.

'Armour-piercing rounds,' said Prototony.

'Not *this* armour,' grunted Tony, shaking off the impact. Though not fatal, it had certainly been jarring enough.

'People are really mean, you know that, T-Star? There's none of this kind of thing at the Cannes Film Festival.'

More shots flew up from below, this time from the right, spinning him left.

'Locate the shooters,' said Tony. 'Do it now.'

He was not worried about the bullets disabling the Iron Man Battle Suit, but it was disturbing that the Mandarin had people in place down there.

I have flown right into the middle of plan B, he realized.

Tracer rounds flew up from below, their pyrotechnic composition burning brightly in the afternoon gloom, and Tony found himself in a swarm of bullets, his dive slowed and nudged off course by the assault.

These guys are good shots, he thought. *I am officially annoyed.*

'How many?' he asked.

'I count three – one in front and two at the rear corners.'

'Show me the first,' said Tony, and Prototony threw up a live feed of a burly man wearing a smog mask and flight goggles. Most of the man was inside the Mandarin's blocker footprint and remained hazy even to the camera.

'He's got something on his back,' said Tony. 'What is that?'

Prototony attempted a zoom, but the image remained stubbornly fuzzy. 'If I had to guess, T-Star, I would say a picnic basket.'

No sooner were the words out than the man executed a vertical liftoff, jet stream bubbling in his wake.

'Or on second thought,' said Prototony, 'it could be a jet pack.'

The Mandarin's man kept firing as he flew, displaying

admirable control of both his weapon and his jet pack and forcing Tony to engage in evasive manoeuvres.

'Gimme a tight spiral sequence,' Tony ordered. 'Take this guy down before he hurts someone.'

Prototony took the wheel, so to speak, corkscrewing Tony around the armed man and analyzing his technology as they drew nearer.

'He's running on jet fuel, T-Star. Highly explosive. Plus he's carrying five hundred rounds in a belt and four incendiary devices.'

So blasting the guy was out. Not that Tony cared much at this precise moment about the fate of one of the Mandarin's goons, but an out-of-control crash trajectory could take the flying thug over the river and into the middle of civilian territory.

'Okay,' he said. 'Let's get up close and personal.'

Tony took the reins and angled himself towards the man, matching his speed and arc. Still the man fired his automatic weapon, until one of his own bullets bounced off Iron Man's chest plate and hit him in the shoulder.

'Moron,' said Tony, without an ounce of pity in his voice. 'Time to land.'

He wrapped the injured man in a bear hug, reaching behind him to crush his fuel line. The jet pack fizzled, and Tony was able to fly the guy down into a mud bank, leaving only his head sticking out.

'That should hold him till the police get here,' he said. 'Now for the other two.'

'They've flown the coop,' said Prototony. 'I'm tracking them across the river, towards downtown.'

Tony actually growled in frustration. The Mandarin was, true to form, prepared to put bystanders in harm's way just to buy himself a few minutes. Well, Iron Man had a trick or two up his sleeve – or in his shoulder panel, to be accurate.

'We need to shrink-wrap these guys while they're still over the river.'

Shrink wrap was slang for the cellophane virus slugs that a bright young Stark employee had come up with for non-lethal takedowns. Once the slug impacted, the virus spread and coated the target with a restrictive layer of cellophane. The cellophane was porous enough to allow shallow breathing, but it had been known to squeeze so tightly that it cracked ribs. On the bright side for the jet-packers, the coating was also buoyant for thirty minutes, until it began to dissolve – probably a little less than thirty minutes in the Thames's acidic water.

'Shrink-wraps in the pipe, T-Star,' said Prototony. 'Two targets, both wearing some kind of jammers. It'll have to be visual targeting.'

Tony hovered, watching the men move closer to a densely populated area.

'Agreed. Visual targeting.'

'So we're going after these guys?'

'No,' said Tony. '*You* are. Transfer yourself into the first missile's onboard systems and then switch out before impact.'

'Boss, I can't leave you alone,' objected Prototony. 'While an AI must obey the orders given by its human, those orders can be countermanded when such orders would allow the human to come to harm.'

Tony would have been touched if he wasn't so insanely angry. 'Really? Earlier, you couldn't wait to get out of the suit. Anyway, those are Asimov's laws, not mine. I'm not big on rules myself.'

'Come on, T-Star. We're a team now; don't send me away. You know that after the final detonation, I'll need a lab reboot.'

'Sometimes a team has gotta split up to take down the bad guys, right? We're in the field now. T-Star and P-Tone, taking out the trash. You ground the jet squad, and I save the girl.'

'Ten-four, partner,' said Prototony, unable to resist this sudden burst of buddyness. He transferred his consciousness to the weapons systems, specifically to the first of two c-virus mini-missiles, which he launched from the Iron Man shoulder ports.

Tony waited until he saw the mini-missiles streak towards their targets, and then he turned his full attention to the fish factory.

I'm coming, Mandarin, he thought. *The past has caught up to you.*

Jet-packer number two was all about the coolness.

I cannot believe how cool I must look just flying up in the sky and stuff, like one of those dinosaurs with wings. A pterodactyl. Yeah, that's it. Pterodactyl Terry.

The man's name was indeed Terry – Terrance McGoomber. He was a Londoner and had long been one of the Mandarin's second-string operatives in the East End. He had worked his way up through a dodgy security firm and a few years of arms smuggling before the Mandarin bailed him out of a jail in Taiwan.

And now here I am flying a jet pack. How cool is that?

'How cool is this?' he shouted in sheer joy, pumping a hundred rounds into the river below him and scattering a flock of haggard grey seagulls.

Terry really should have kept his mouth shut, because the c-virus shell hit him in the side of the face and sent him spinning onto the riverbank, where the cellophane quickly crawled over his body like an aggressive translucent octopus. And because of his wide-open bragging mouth, he ended up swallowing a large blob of the material and was constipated for a month.

Jet-packer number three got a little farther, because she was made of more dogged stuff than Pterodactyl Terry. In fact, she was Terry's fiancée and was in proud possession of a fake diamond engagement ring and the quite splendid name Summer Berry, which would be enough to make most men fall in love, and Terry was no exception. Summer and Terry were supposed to be starting their honeymoon on this very day, but the Mandarin had messed up those plans by calling in his B-team to stake out a stinking fish factory on the Thames. The place had no conveniences. Even Starbucks hadn't bothered to set up shop out there. Summer was fed up, but she kept that to herself. The Mandarin didn't approve of lip, and the money he paid would see them through the first ten years of their marriage.

I'll do the job, thought Summer as she crested the Thames bank and took aim at a wedding party outside the Duck and Dive Pub. *But if my wedding day is ruined, so is everyone else's.*

This was the last semirational thought she would have for a while, because at that moment the c-virus slug struck her square in the back of her helmet, splurging onto the communications module. Just before she got wrapped up tight and deposited in four feet of sludge by the riverbank to be pecked at by desultory seagulls, Summer could have sworn she heard a tinny voice say, 'Mission completed, T-Star. P-Tone, peace out.'

As an aside, the wedding couple below became minor celebrities when they recorded the entire attempted attack and even fished Summer out of the sludge. The bride was heard to say, 'This was the best wedding ever. Beyond my wildest dreams.' And the groom would later go on to win *Celebrity MasterChef*.

Tony blasted through the factory's skylight and did a quick

circuit of the building, too fast for anyone without a target locking system to get a bead on him. He needn't have bothered with the fancy flying, because the Mandarin was lounging on a totally out-of-place purple velvet sofa set squarely in the centre of the main chamber, apparently paying little attention to the drama he had caused. Saoirse sat beside him, looking equal parts surly and terrified, which is a hybrid expression that only teenagers can pull off. Between them sat the Party Pack helmet, its expression only slightly less bored than the Mandarin's.

This was confusing behaviour on the Mandarin's part. Surely he should be doing his little combat disco dance or at the very least holding Saoirse by the throat and threatening to kill her if Tony came any closer. Tony ran a thermal imaging scan but could not penetrate the Mandarin's blocker. There were no other visible threats, which almost certainly meant that there were hidden threats somewhere.

Tony throttled back and touched down ten feet from the man who had murdered his friend. He knew that were it not for Saoirse, he would simply blast over and throttle the terrorist. But his respect for the man's sneakiness gave him pause. So he simply stood there fuming, waiting for the Mandarin to launch into his monologue. He did not have to wait long.

'Thank you, Mr Tony Stark, for your respect,' said the Mandarin, clinking those accursed rings off each other like some kind of deadly executive toy.

'Respect?' said Tony. 'You think I respect you?'

'You respect my intellect and my abilities. Otherwise I think you would have already tried to kill me.'

'I respect Saoirse and *her* intellect. And I bet a low-life murderer like you will have set up some kind of trap where the kid gets it if I do anything. Am I right?'

'You are on the right track,' admitted the Mandarin. 'I wish to finish our combat from the island. But not like this. Not while you wear the suit.'

'Man to man, right?'

'That is correct.'

'Now why would I do that?'

The Mandarin rapped on the side of Saoirse's head, which is about the most annoying thing you can do to teenagers aside from telling them to *calm down*.

'Tell him, child,' he said. 'Tell Mr Tony Stark why he must fight me.'

Saoirse lifted her chin and Tony could see now that whatever the Mandarin had done to her, she had put up a fight. Her face was scraped, both eyes were puffy, and she was missing a front tooth.

'Big Mr Mandarin tagged me with his stupid ring,' she said belligerently, showing it on her finger. But just below the belligerence there was an undercurrent of desperation. 'It's got some kind of tightening mechanism.'

Tony flexed and a dozen smart missiles sprouted on his shoulders.

'An interesting reaction,' said the Mandarin. 'You

plan to burn the ring. Unfortunately, that would kill the wearer, too. I doubt your missiles are so smart they can target just one ring.'

'Tell me what's in it!' he demanded.

'A shaped charge coded to my biometrics. If I die, she dies. There is also a proximity alert, and a timer. The girl has about five minutes to live, much less if she attempts to leave this building. My signal jammers don't affect my own technology.'

'Five minutes?' said Tony. 'If you wanted this showdown, then why the jet-pack guys?'

'I had hoped you would spend your famous c-virus rounds. Which you did. I am so happy we two titans are talking, Tony Stark. But the girl has three hundred seconds only.'

'Squash him, Stark,' said Saoirse defiantly. 'Squash him flat, then go save my sister in Fourni.'

'That is an option,' said the Mandarin. 'Take your revenge on me and let the girl die. Or ...'

'Or we fight? Correct?'

'Yes. Come out of the suit and fight me. Once I have dispatched you, then I deactivate the ring.'

Tony felt he had to ask: 'And if I win?'

'If you can force me to yield, then I will also deactivate the ring. You have my word. And please, Tony Stark, do not attempt to hack my rings. They are coded to my biometrics and on a network closed more tightly than the fist of God.'

'So you keep your wonderful rings? Hardly a fair fight.'

'Of course not. We fight as my ancestors did. Fists and fury. That means you remove your college ring also.'

Tony removed a gauntlet and tugged off his ring, his blood boiling. This hateful person was infuriating. It was almost unbelievable to him that the man who claimed to have killed his friend was within reach and not only was Tony not repeatedly punching his smug face, but he was contemplating getting into an unfair fight in which he himself was likely to be beaten to death.

But what choice did he have?

There must be a way out. He couldn't think. There was no time.

'Tick-tock,' said the Mandarin melodramatically. Then, as though taking Tony's decision for granted, he stood and stripped off his gown, revealing his muscular torso with its dragon tattoo.

'Nice ink,' said Tony. 'Prison?' But the jab was not delivered with his usual jauntiness, possibly because it was hurled at this particular man at this particular time.

The Mandarin wagged his finger like a metronome pendulum. The message was clear: five minutes would soon be four.

'All right, all right,' said Tony, stepping out of the armour, which reverse-telescoped away from his limbs as he moved. For his part, the Mandarin tugged off his nine remaining rings and built a neat tower on the arm of the sofa.

'I will relish this, Stark. No trickery this time. Just two men destined to wage war on each other.'

No trickery, thought Tony. *I doubt that very much.*

Truth be told, he could use a little trickery of his own about now. Although he had been patched up pretty well in the *Tanngrisnir*'s sick bay, he was still crocked in the lower-limbs department, and his shoulder felt as raw as a bloody steak where the Mandarin had cut into it in their last fight.

Not exactly peak fitness.

The Mandarin gestured at the two transparent casts wrapped around Tony's legs.

'I had thought that your legs must be shattered.'

'They were, but don't worry, I can still lick you, buddy.'

The Mandarin finished limbering up. 'Air casts?'

'Yeah,' lied Tony. 'Can we get on with this? Tick-tock, right?'

'Most assuredly, Mr Tony Stark,' said the Mandarin. 'Before we begin, just remember that I murdered your paramour.'

Rational, laid-back man that Tony was, this comment turned him into a raging gorilla, and he rushed at the Mandarin, forgetting every lesson Rhodey had ever taught him, chief among them being that outside the suit he was just a normal guy.

The Mandarin sidestepped the attack with ludicrous

ease and finger-jabbed Tony in the solar plexus on his way past. The sharp pain brought Tony back to his senses, but it was probably too late, because, contrary to what the movies teach us, in hand-to-hand combat one good blow usually decides the outcome. The Mandarin spun on his toes and pursued Tony, landing several chops on his damaged shoulder. There was no banter or discussion. The Mandarin was all business on this occasion and would not allow his prey to escape once more. With each blow Tony sank lower until he was down on one knee panting, with blood streaming from his injured shoulder.

Anna, he thought. *I have failed you.*

For a crazy moment it seemed that he saw Anna's face in the factory floor dust, and though he knew it was just his exhausted mind playing tricks, it gave him the strength to fight on.

The Mandarin locked his hands and raised them overhead for a finishing strike to the back of his opponent's exposed neck, when the opponent did something that should not have been possible except on the surface of the moon.

Tony somehow leaped six feet straight up and spun in the air, sweeping his right leg in a roundhouse kick that took the Mandarin straight in the teeth. In truth, the blow hurt Tony almost as much as it hurt the Mandarin, but Tony had the satisfaction of seeing the pain on his mortal enemy's face.

The Mandarin's strong teeth bit deep into the cast,

and gas flooded his mouth. Tony suddenly lost his altitude, and both men went down in a heap. The Mandarin spat out plastic and crawled away.

'That is no ordinary cast,' he said, and Saoirse burst out laughing, for the Mandarin's voice was that of a chipmunk.

'That is no ordinary cast,' she squeaked. 'I'd say there was some helium in there.'

Which explained why Tony could jump so high.

Tony used his remaining cast to spring himself across the factory floor and pounce on the Mandarin.

'Now,' he said, grabbing the Mandarin by the throat, 'you will release the girl.'

The Mandarin said nothing, so Tony punched him in his smug face, maybe half a dozen times, each blow sending shockwaves down the length of his own fractured legs.

'Let her go!' he shouted. 'This is over!'

The Mandarin declared, 'Nothing is over, Tony Stark!' which might have sounded ominous had it not been for the helium squeak.

But as he said this, the Mandarin stretched out his arms and separated his fingers – for all the good *that* would do him, one might think – but on the arm of the sofa, the stack of rings rattled and quivered.

'No!' said Saoirse. 'Boss, look out!'

One by one the rings lifted into the air. They formed a revolving circle before zooming over to drop neatly onto the Mandarin's waiting fingers.

'Coded to my biometrics,' he said, his voice back to normal. 'Now this is truly over.'

The Mandarin's thumb ring flashed, and from its crystal grew a flower of white light that sprawled across the terrorist's hand, creating in effect a glove of power.

'You see? I, too, have a gauntlet,' he said, and he brought the armed hand up to strike Tony in the temple.

The effect was staggering. Tony was knocked clean across the room. He crashed through an old cabinet and into the solid wall. Dust and plaster showered on top of him when he fell to the floor, bleeding from his ears. It was clear that the Mandarin's strength had been considerably magnified by the mysterious white light, and it was equally apparent that even if by some miracle Tony rallied, he would not survive a second blow.

'Now, Tony Stark,' said the Mandarin, 'you fought dishonorably, and that is how you shall die. I would like you to know that I have no intention of freeing the girl. So die in the full knowledge of your failure to avenge your beloved and rescue the damsel in distress.'

Tony managed to roll over onto his back, and the effort sent sharp bolts of pain shooting through his chest.

The Mandarin loomed over him, holding out his enhanced fist. 'Do you like my new technology? It may further infuriate you to know that Anna Wei developed the white-light ring.'

Tony coughed and it felt as though his lungs had come

loose from their moorings.

'Let the girl go, Mandarin,' he said. 'Show some humanity.'

The Mandarin smiled though bloodied teeth. 'That's just the thing, Mr Tony Stark. I despise humanity.'

And his hand came down. But before it could do more than graze Tony's chest, the Mandarin was knocked sideways slightly as Saoirse butted him in the midriff, which would have had no impact at all had she not been wearing the Party Pack Iron Man helmet. As it was, the impact was minimal, and the Mandarin simply reached down with his free hand and planted it on the crown of the helmet.

'Enough, child,' he said, grunting to dislodge the girl as she wrapped her hands around his waist. 'Your time is running out.'

Saoirse held on for a good ten seconds before the Mandarin put his shoulder into it and pushed her across the room. Tony watched the girl roll in the dirt and thought that he would prefer to spend his last moment looking at Saoirse rather than the Mandarin. It was almost unbearable that the man who killed Anna was about to kill him and then the Irish girl.

Saoirse tumbled in the dust and raised the Iron Man visor. The face that appeared should have been despondent, but instead Saoirse's expression was fierce and victorious. Looking Tony straight in the eye, she very deliberately took off the Mandarin's ring.

'Hey, Mandy,' she said, tossing the ring to him. 'Catch.'

It would take a strong and focused person to resist a cry of *catch*, and the Mandarin was not as focused as he might have been. Instinctively, he reached up to snatch the twinkling ring out of the air.

He looked at the ring in his hand and did not understand what was happening. 'My ring. Mine.'

'That's right, your ring.'

'But . . .' said the Mandarin. 'But . . .'

Tony finished the sentence for him. 'But how?'

How had Saoirse removed the ring?

Saoirse made a *duh* face at him and pointed at the Party Pack helmet. And then Tony, being a genius, got it.

When the Mandarin put his hand on the helmet, Saoirse downloaded his biometrics and synced with the rings. She controls them now.

About half a second later, the Mandarin got the idea and dropped the explosive ring like a hot coal. He looked down fearfully at his other rings, but he couldn't do anything without letting go of Tony's chest.

'No!' he said. 'It's not possible.'

Then one of his rings activated and sent an electrical shock through his body. And from him into Tony.

'Friday!' said Tony when his jaw loosened. 'What are you doing?'

'I don't know specifically,' said Saoirse. 'I activated them all.'

This was good news in that Tony was alive to hear

it but bad in that one of the rings was explosive – at least one.

The Mandarin confirmed Tony's worry. 'What have you done, child? There's an impact beam on my index ring.'

It's incredible how two words can motivate the most exhausted person, and the words *impact beam* are right up there with *beware shark* for getting someone up and moving. Tony bucked and wriggled until he was free of the Mandarin. Then he grabbed his enemy's hand.

'Let me help you,' he said, attempting to straighten the Mandarin's index finger. 'An impact beam will hit like TNT.'

The Mandarin lashed out, scything the air with an icy blade from his left hand. 'Never, Stark. Never will I bow to you.'

Saoirse pulled Tony, yanking him clear of the sheet of ice.

'Come on,' she said. 'We need to –'

'Exit quickly,' said Tony. 'And I know a man who can fly. An Iron Man.'

Saoirse grabbed Tony's elbow and dragged him along. 'Quickly, boss. Suit up.'

The suit stood where Tony had left it, yawning open as though an alien had burst through the chest.

'Protocol thirteen!' he shouted. 'Envelope.'

The suit jerked to life, used its fourteen cameras to precisely locate Tony Stark and seemed to drop on him like a knocked-over suit of armour. But the suit's fall was scientific and accurate, and moments later it was a second skin on the billionaire inventor.

'Climb on,' he said to Saoirse. 'There are handles on the upper back.'

But Saoirse was already there. She knew the Iron Man system inside out, and by the time Tony had finished the command, she was clamped on and ready to go.

'Fly, boss!' she called. 'Fly!'

Tony did not need to be told twice – though she *had* told him twice – and he blasted off towards the busted roof panel.

'Hold on,' he said, and he piloted the suit to a safe distance over the fish factory. His last sight of the Mandarin before a churning explosion filled the factory's every corner was on the monitor from the suit's rear camera. The Mandarin was tearing off the remaining rings and hurling them from him. It might have been a trick of the gloom, but it seemed as though the Mandarin looked skywards into the camera and shouted, 'Soon, Tony Stark!'

He would have to have his lip-reading software analyze that later.

Then the explosion shook the factory to its foundations, Saoirse screamed and Tony forgot all about the Mandarin's last words – if they *were* his last words.

The wreck of the *Tanngrisnir*

Diavolo Conroy was still lying on the bridge of the

Tanngrisnir ten minutes later when Iron Man descended slowly through the hole made by Freddie Leveque.

Tony Stark flipped up his faceplate and could not hide his dismay as the sheer scale of the devastation sank in.

'Not a scratch, Conroy. I did say that, didn't I?'

Conroy did not bother getting up. In fact, he didn't even have the strength to open his eyes. 'Yep, I do recall something along those lines, but things got out of hand.'

Tony noticed Leveque. 'You took out Freddie. How the hell did you manage that?'

'I had a stick,' said Diavolo.

'A stick?'

'I had a ball, too. Not just a stick.'

'Well, that explains it.'

'It was a hurley, I bet,' said a girl with a slight lisp.

Conroy opened his eyes and climbed to his feet to see a teenage girl on Iron Man's back. The girl's face was soot streaked and her hair looked like an electrical current had recently passed through it. She had nasty shiners coming up around both eyes and seemed to be missing a front tooth.

'You'd be Saoirse, I suppose. Good to see you safe and sound.'

'Thanks to me,' said Tony. 'Credit where it's due.'

'Credit?' said Diavolo. 'The poor child is in worse shape than this boat. And you have her flying around on your back?'

'In my defence, there are some handles back there,'

said Tony.

'I would be surprised if her parents don't sue you, Stark. Once the United Nations get through with you.'

'Luckily for me, Saoirse doesn't have parents,' said Tony. 'Oh, wait – that was insensitive, wasn't it?'

Saoirse slapped his armoured shoulder. 'Yes, it was, boss. Very.'

Conroy took out his smartphone to call a doctor, then realized that it was just as fried as the rest of the boat's instruments.

'I suppose we'll just have to find a doctor the old-fashioned way,' he said, tossing his phone onto a heap of smoldering electronics. Conroy helped Saoirse down from the Iron Man suit. He pointed to her mouth. 'Do you still have the tooth?'

Saoirse grimaced. 'I swallowed it.'

'I don't suppose you've got a machine that can fix teeth, Tony boy?'

'If I did, it's junk now, along with the rest of my gear.'

'Shiv, my wife, will think of something,' Conroy assured Saoirse.

Stark grinned. '*Shiv.* You do know that your wife's name is slang for –'

'I know. A concealed blade.'

'Wait a minute,' said Saoirse. 'Why would your wife be getting involved?'

'Because you are a minor without any guardians as far as I can see. So you stay in our spare room tonight. And you' – he turned to Tony – 'sleep on the couch. I have questions for you both.'

'Come on, Diavolo,' said Tony. 'I've had a rough night, saving the environment and so forth. I need five-star accommodations.'

'That's *Inspector Conroy* to you,' said Diavolo. 'And our couch *is* five stars. There'll be tea and toast in it for you if I like the answers to my questions.'

Stark jerked a thumb upward. 'I could just fly away. I'd be stateside before you could get the word out.'

Conroy looked him squarely in the eye. 'You could do that, Tony, but I would think less of you.'

Saoirse laughed. 'I like this fella, boss. He knows your weak spots.'

'There's a lot of that going around,' said Tony. 'I'm the one wearing the armour here, but I feel like a soft touch.'

The three talked and bonded a little bit and were all mightily relieved that they hadn't allowed untold tragedy to come to pass. But things could have gone a whole different way, because Spin Zhuk was watching the entire touching tableau through a starboard porthole, thinking, *They are so fat-faced with their smugness. Stark's mask is open, and I have a shot.*

And she would have taken that shot, because even though the Mandarin had been a cruel master, Spin Zhuk was a loyal soldier. She could only presume that Iron Man had killed the Mandarin, and he must pay for his crime.

But then her communicator vibrated in her pocket, and it was a most significant vibrating pattern. SOS – save our souls.

The master is alive, she realized. But if he was sending the SOS code, he was injured and needed her immediately.

I will follow the locator on my communicator, Spin decided, and it would be prudent to do so without security forces on her tail.

'Another time, Iron Man,' she whispered. 'Another time.'

For now, Spin Zhuk was content to hike across country as far as Dublin Busáras, where she had a fully equipped go-bag in locker forty-two.

By sunset that evening Spin Zhuk was on the ferry to Holyhead, watching reports of her own failed mission on Sky News.

EPILOGUE

The tiny island of Fourni had for centuries been considered the gateway to West Africa. Nestled in the equatorial Gulf of Guinea, the country enjoyed the cool night breezes from the Atlantic but avoiding the worst of the Saharan glare. Once a French colony, Fourni had achieved its independence in 1956 and had avoided the all-too-common afflictions of the African continent – dictatorships, political corruption and military coups – largely because of the strength of both its ancient people and its economy. In the previous decade, however, like much of the planet, Fourni had fallen on hard times.

The general impact of the world depression on its export market was compounded by the confusion of its aging president and the influx of asylum-seekers from neighbouring countries. The capital, Port Verdé, was hit hardest, and many of the wealthier citizens literally fled in the night, fearing that their assets might be seized should they wait for a total collapse.

In the past eighteen months, the National Democratic Party had taken power, with the charismatic Adama Demel assuming the presidency, and huge steps had already been made to restore Fourni to its proper place as a world centre of trade, arts and freedom. But the country had a long, hard road ahead of it and tensions were high with bordering nations; so it was definitely not the time for a symbol of some superpower to go sticking his nose in. That was why Iron Man had refused Saoirse's request in the first place, but now he felt a little different about things, which was why he dropped in on Adama Demel before making a move on what had been the Port Verdé Girls Home.

The president of Fourni, who occupied two small rooms in the massive presidential palace and had turned the rest over to the poor, awoke that night to find the American Iron Man standing at the foot of his bed.

Iron Man spoke in unaccented but flawed Fournese, saying, 'Do not be made of alarms. I have not come here to place you in a harem.'

Demel reached to his nightstand for his glasses to make

sure he was seeing what he thought he was seeing. Having confirmed that, he said in English, 'I think English, don't you, Mr Stark? Your translator needs a little tweaking.'

Tony opened his faceplate. 'I appreciate it, Mr President. We would save ourselves a lot of confusion.'

Demel turned on his bedside light and sat up calmly in bed. If it had occurred to him that this armoured figure could blow up the entire palace if he felt like it, it didn't show on his face.

'And what can I do for the famous Iron Man?' he asked.

Tony ordered the suit to sit in midair, because if he sat on the room's wicker chair, it would collapse into splinters.

'I need a visa,' he said. 'And I thought if I explained the situation to you directly, it could save months of misunderstandings and media hysteria.'

Adama Demel smiled. 'Actually, you are already in the country, Mr Stark. But if I ignore that technicality, then a visa for how long?'

'Maybe ten minutes. Half an hour, tops.'

'And for what purpose?'

Tony went through the whole thing: how Liz Tory had come with the Red Cross and helped build the Port Verdé Girls Home and how she was now a prisoner there.

'And what I thought is, I would drop in and airlift the girl to safety. And in return, Stark Industries would commit –'

Demel's eyes hardened and he raised a hand. 'No, Mr Stark. My country will accept nothing in exchange for the safety of a girl. Here in Fourni we were building temples and writing philosophy while the Greeks were scrabbling around in the mud. Our most famous philosopher, Mother Abba, once said, "Every daughter is mother of the earth."'

'Cool,' said Tony, which seemed lame even to him, but Demel approved.

'Yes, cool. It is cool. Exactly so. Now go, Mr Stark. Retrieve this daughter of Ireland. I will be generous. You have one hour if you can promise me that not a soul will be injured.'

'You have my word,' said Tony.

'Excellent, then this never happened unless it needs to have happened, if you see what I mean.'

'I think I do,' said Tony, closing his faceplate.

'Then fly, Mr Stark. I have a meeting with the UK ambassador at first light and I need my eight hours.'

Tony was gone before Demel's head hit the pillow.

'Cool?' said Saoirse Tory in his ear. 'I can't believe President Demel quoted Mother Abba and you said *cool.*'

Tony flew low and fast through the winding ramshackle streets of Port Verdé, the Atlantic Ocean twinkling in the starlight off his port side.

'Mother Abba? Didn't she do "Dancing Queen"?'

'Stop opening your mouth, boss,' said Saoirse.

'It's letting you down.'

On Tony's heads-up display, the girls home pulsed softly less than three miles southeast on the fringe of the city.

'I am doing this for you, Saoirse,' he reminded the girl who was again operating as his onboard AI, for this mission only. 'You could be nice to me.'

'You're buying off your conscience. And you *attempted* to buy off President Demel. That was such a cringe fest. I told you it wouldn't work.'

'It's worked on a lotta presidents before now,' said Tony, though he would have to admit if pressed that Demel's expression had made him feel like a bit of a sleaze.

'Coming up on the home now,' said Saoirse, suddenly all business. 'Adjusting height to fifty yards and powering back to minimum thrusters. Do you want to penguin in?'

'Not tonight,' said Tony. 'I'm going to swoop. Much more dramatic. Give me full manual.'

'Full manual. Roger that, if you're certain.'

'I am certain,' confirmed Tony. 'And can you run a full range of scans? Just to make sure there aren't some terrorists hiding under tarps, or anything like that.'

Saoirse groaned. 'Wow, that's only the tenth time you've brought that up this trip. When are you going to let it go?'

'Never,' said Tony. 'Never, ever, ever. That's blackmail gold right there.'

'Full thermal,' said Saoirse through gritted teeth. 'We have three dozen warm humanoids. Several blades and

I have recognition on one AK-47 assault rifle. No bullets or firing pin.'

'That's how I like my assault rifles,' said Tony. 'Going in. Stand by to be deliriously happy and in my emotional debt for the rest of your life.'

'Thanks, boss,' said Saoirse, and she meant it.

*

Things did not go exactly as planned. The initial 'shock and awe' part worked out well, but then things took an unexpected turn.

Tony swooped in, lights blazing and thrusters roaring, and landed in the small yard behind the building, sending guinea fowls gobbling for cover and raising spirals of dust in the air. The effect of his arrival was instant: boys streamed from the doors and windows of the modest building, armed with clubs and knives. With the customary fearlessness of youth they attacked Iron Man, raining down bonging blows on his armour.

'Come on, boys,' said Tony through his speakers. 'You might as well be ants attacking a rhino. Seriously, you're embarrassing yourselves.'

That was what he thought he had said, but because he was using his bug-ridden translator, what he actually said was, 'Wonderful, rhinoceros. It is seriously the ants who are coming.'

Which made the boys fall back and wonder if perhaps this was Iron Man's stupid cousin who was attacking them.

'I don't think you said what you think you said,' said

Saoirse. 'This translator is so bad. You should try my app.'

'You mean bad like dope?' said Tony hopefully.

'I definitely mean *dope*. We agree on that.'

'It doesn't matter. Words don't mean anything to these youngsters. Tasteless though it is, I have to throw a scare into the leader. Now which one do you think that is?'

From her new bedroom in the Dublin house where the Conroy's were fostering her, Saoirse cycled through Iron Man's cameras. 'I would think it's the guy pointing the AK-47 at you.'

Tony spotted him. 'No bullets, right?'

'Right.'

'Okay. Let's give this guy a glimpse of hell.'

'You are such a drama queen, boss.'

Tony set the eye socket lights to glow red and added a few filters to his voice box until he sounded like a cross between a lion and an orc. Then he advanced on the armed boy, speaking rapidly.

Though the boys could never distinguish individual words with all the feedback and reverb, what Tony was actually doing was singing Abba's "Dancing Queen," because it was in his head. Only Saoirse could hear the unfiltered version.

'Seriously?' she said. 'I am trying to work here.'

'Friday night and the lights are low,' growled Tony. *'Looking out for a place to go.'*

As he said this, Iron Man advanced rapidly on the gang leader, who seemed to grow smaller as Tony approached.

'I shoot,' cried the boy, waving an assault rifle that he was barely able to lift. 'I shoot.'

Iron Man roared in anger (*'You are the dancing queen, young and sweet, only seventeen'*) and crushed the AK's barrel with the fingers of his gauntlet. Then, for good measure, he put a blast from his palm repulsor into the earth at the boy's shoeless feet. The boy was not harmed, unless you count scorched leg hairs, but the defiance drained from his face.

'There's Liz,' said Saoirse in Tony's ear. 'Grab her and go.'

'Just a second,' said Tony. 'I'm just gonna fly this guy up a thousand feet and pretend to drop him.'

'What do you think you are doing?' came a strident voice that was very similar to Saoirse's but even bossier, if such a level of bossiness was even possible.

Tony looked over the terrified boy's shoulder and saw a taller version of Saoirse, red hair pulled back in a severe bun, dressed much the same as the others in earth-toned T-shirt and pants.

'Liz?' he asked, switching off his translator. 'Liz Tory. Finally. Grab hold of the grips on my back. We are outta here. No need for thanks yet.'

If Tony was expecting sobbing gratitude, then he was to be disappointed. If anything, Liz Tory seemed more furious than her kidnappers had been.

'I asked you, what in heaven's name do you think you are doing? That poor boy is scared witless.'

Tony patted the boy's head. 'I think you mean that

poor *kidnapper* is scared witless.'

'Kidnapper?' said Liz, incredulous. 'Ahmed a kidnapper? Who told you that?'

Saoirse whispered in Tony's ear. 'She's really angry. You might have made a mistake.'

'Me?' said Tony. '*I* might have made a mistake?'

'Is Saoirse in there?' said Liz. 'This has her blundering style written all over it. Sending in her mechanical goon.'

'Hey,' said Tony. 'Iron Man has feelings, too. I'm no one's goon.'

'Just grab her,' said Saoirse. 'We can explain later.'

Tony took one step forward and Liz raised her fist. 'Don't touch me, Iron Man. You leave us alone. We're doing just fine without you.'

Doing just fine? thought Tony. *That doesn't sound like the terrified babbling of a kidnap victim. And I should know; I've done my share of terrified babbling.*

Now that he looked around him, the small compound did not seem like the hideout of a desperate gang. The garden was well tended, and the interior walls had been freshly painted. There was even a mural of happy children holding hands.

'Okay, Saoirse,' he said, 'I'm thinking you two need to have a face to face.' Before Saoirse could object, he projected her webcam image onto the perimeter wall.

Saoirse, the heretofore toughest kid in the universe, immediately welled up.

'Liz! You're okay. You're alive. It's so good to see you.'

Liz also dropped the Tory attitude. 'You too, Sis. How's Granddad?'

That was the waterworks question, and Saoirse broke down sobbing. 'He's gone, Liz. Over a year now. In his sleep. He made me promise to get you out.'

Tony sat on the ground and was joined by three dozen children, who watched the video call as though it were a movie.

'Oh no,' said Liz. 'Poor Granddad. And poor you, you're all alone.' Then she frowned. '*Get me out?* What do you mean, get me out? My work is here.'

'It's okay, Liz,' said Saoirse, wiping her cheeks. 'I'm not alone. I have Diavolo and Shiv. And the goon is mine, too. You don't need to be afraid of these boys now.'

Liz snorted. 'Afraid of these boys? They should be scared of *me*, if their chores aren't done.'

'But they kidnapped you, right? Threw out the girls?'

'No. They *protect* the girls. We all protect each other.'

'But the orphanage director said the home was overrun by a street gang and they kept you on as a hostage.'

'Ha!' crowed Liz. 'The director? Serge? That lying fraud was skimming all the money you sent. The entire staff was on the take. And worse, they were forcing the girls to work for a local sweatshop. So we staged a coup and brought in the orphans' siblings. Now we look after each other and I am their nurse.'

'But the aid office?'

'Serge is still lying to them and taking their money.

Port Verdé doesn't have Internet – it barely has electricity most days – so I couldn't get word out. I sent letters, but Serge must have intercepted them. That guy pays off everybody.'

Saoirse persisted with her one-track message. 'You have to come home, Liz.'

'This is home now,' said Liz Tory. 'These kids need me.'

'You're barely more than a kid yourself.'

'I'm twenty, which is middle-aged here. I need one more year; let's agree to that. President Demel is making great strides. Ahmed and I can hold this place together for one more year with your help.'

'I've been sending the funds from the app,' said Saoirse. 'Every month. The director said the kidnappers would kill you if I didn't.'

Liz shrieked with anger. 'Saoirse! You are so gullible.'

'I've told her that,' said Tony. 'She falls for every sob story.'

'The director keeps all the money,' explained Liz. 'The orphanage doesn't see a penny. We need medical supplies and cash in small packages.'

'Mr Stark could do that,' said Saoirse's big head on the wall. 'He owes me big time. I'm gonna revolutionize his company.'

'Sure,' said Tony. 'I owe Saoirse so much because of all the favours she's done for me. I am so deep in the debt hole it's not even funny.'

'I need small packages,' Liz repeated, ignoring the rampant sarcasm. 'If clunky bum here is spotted flying in, the game will be up. Serge will send his men to investigate. For now, Serge needs to think no one is onto him and his money is safe.'

'Clunky bum?' said Tony. 'No fair. This suit is sleek and streamlined.'

And it occurred to him not for the first time that Irish people were very good at finding a person's weak spots.

'There must be another way of flying aid in?' said Saoirse, and both sisters fixed Tony with their green-eyed gazes.

'Wow,' said Tony. 'Pressure. Irish eyes ain't smiling so much as shooting death rays.'

'Come on, clunky,' said Liz, rapping his helmet, much to the amusement of the orphans. 'Anyone in there? You must have some toys laying about.'

'Toys …' said Tony, and at the mere sound of the word, he was transported back through the decades to his father's office. That afternoon all those years ago, when Annabel the secretary had been so teed-off with him for taking her daughter, Cissy – no, *Cecilia* – to see the dolphin.

Inside the helmet Tony closed his eyes and remembered their visit to the beach. He could feel the warm wind off the Pacific; he could hear the squeals floating down from the Ferris wheel.

My hair. My god, it was magnificent.

Then Howard Stark entered the flashback and Tony felt his stomach lurch and sink.

Why wouldn't you ever listen, Dad?

Tony Stark was smart enough to know that the reason he'd pursued Stark Industries' weapons program so vigorously was because of his parents' untimely deaths and because of the promise his dad had extracted from him.

'I promise, Dad,' he'd said. 'No toys, just weapons.'

And right then, Tony had stopped being a boy.

Now Tony was more certain than ever that he must do more than rid the world of the weapons created by Stark Industries; he must continue to be an active force for peace.

It is not enough
To fill the hole.
But climb the hill
To win your soul.

And with his resolve stronger than ever, Tony Stark felt a little lighter, as if the power of determination had lifted a weight from his shoulders.

He opened his eyes and saw that the Tory sisters were still skewering him with their emerald eyeballs. The orphans were regarding him with some interest, as though he were a space robot – all except Ahmed, who was trying to straighten the barrel of his AK.

'Well, boss?' said the big-headed projection of Saoirse.

'Do you have anything that can get medicines in here without alerting Serge?'

Tony blinked a command and raised the Iron Man faceplate. He was almost immediately bitten by a mosquito, but he ignored it because the suit would jab him with antihistamine to prevent swelling.

He took a deep breath of sweet night air and said, 'Yeah, I got something. A swarm of somethings, actually. Tiny little suckers. They'll fly in here right under this Serge guy's nose and he won't know a thing about it.'

On the wall, Saoirse's image nodded in appreciation. 'I think I know where you're going, boss.'

'And I know where *you're* going. Trinity College, to get an actual doctorate.'

Saoirse groaned. 'Come on. We talked about this. Those guys are so last century. They wouldn't know a pentaquark if it bit them on the nose.'

'Nevertheless, I only employ qualified people. So if you want to work for me, then you'd better hit the books.'

Saoirse's face shifted through several expressions, which made it look like she was trying to blow up an invisible balloon. She eventually settled on grudging acceptance, which is very close in appearance to long-term constipation.

'Okay, boss,' she said. 'I'll do a doctorate. Two, at most. Shouldn't take more than a year.'

'By which time Liz will be home,' said Tony. 'So double celebration.'

Liz used the mention of her name to introduce herself into the conversation.

'This is all great, how you two are bonding and all, but we were talking about a delivery system. Remember?'

'That is right,' said Tony. 'I feel like helping you guys out, even trigger-happy Ahmed.'

'What's the system? How does it work?'

'I call them TOTs. Tiny insectoids that can fox any surveillance. Disposable, too, and biodegradable. Once they drop their package, they become playthings for the kids. No one will ever weaponize these babies.'

Liz frowned. 'Are you talking about drones? But drones *are* weapons.'

'They *used* to be weapons,' said Tony, and his heart felt happier just saying the words. To go with his lightness of heart, he flashed a smile that was brighter and more genuine than any of the thousands he had produced for the world's media. 'But now they're toys.'

And rightly feeling that he could not top this statement as his parting words, Tony Stark pulled down his faceplate, switched to flight mode, and shot like a reverse falling star into the African sky.

As a farewell gift, he dropped a pod webcam into the garden, and Saoirse's face stayed on the wall beside the mural so the sisters could talk every day until he got a satellite phone to Liz in the first TOT shipment. Saoirse's face still wore the not very attractive long-term constipation look, which made Tony chuckle as he flew away.